ARCANE CONNECTION

Arcane Connection

L.A. Binley

Paperback ISBN: 978-1-7399673-3-8
E-Book ISBN : 978-1-7399673-2-1

Cover design by GetCovers.com
Edited By: Turner Alpha and Edits, Karen Sanders Editing, and Proofreading by Mich

Typeset in Garamond

First Edition: July 2025

10 9 8 7 6 5 4 3 2 1
Labinley.com

*For Violet, you make me want to achieve all my
dreams to show you it's possible.*

Also by L.A. Binley

Artefact 299

Chapter One

The wind whipped Viola's hair around her face. No matter how many times she moved the strands, they found their way back to the crevice of her mouth. The dark strands shadowed her features, changing her appearance in the dimming light of the day.

"One day, I'll chop this off—" she muttered to herself.

A quick flash of light steadied her feet at the edge of the road. The car whooshed by before she continued. She glanced at the time on her phone, eyebrows furrowed as she calculated how impossible it would be to do a ten-minute walk in only three.

"I am not going to be my mum's favourite person tonight, or maybe this week."

Her pace quickened. The usual carefree gait was replaced with a cross between a power walk and a jog. Inch by inch, she closed in on her destination. She hadn't wanted to be a part of the coven. She hadn't wanted to join in with the initiation. Ever since her dad had sacrificed himself, the rest of their group had neglected Viola and her mum. Why would she want to go through with the farce of being initiated and accepted into their circle? It wouldn't change anyone's opinion of them. The entire decision felt like a pantomime.

She stumbled through the protective barrier around the house, the wind leaving her hair alone. She smoothed out what she could, attempting to eliminate as many kinks and knots as possible before brushing her knuckles over the wooden door. She waited. She knocked again, louder than before. She waited.

"Fine, I'll do it your way," she said to no one in particular.

Viola drew herself back and concentrated on the energy humming inside her. It was typical of the coven to introduce a test to be able to get into the meeting. It wasn't something she had heard of happening for a while, but she wouldn't put it past the Elders to do this the year she was due to join their ranks. Focusing on the power inside her, she felt for anything out of the ordinary. It wasn't often a witch would be able to feel leftover magic, but it hadn't stopped her before.

The energy rushed over her. She focused its attention on the door in front of her. It hummed along her outstretched arm. She felt it hovering above her fingertips. Her energy inspected each section of the door, prodding and poking for any flaws or hint of what might have been left behind. Viola almost gave up hope until she felt a shudder. Her eyes narrowed. She concentrated on the edge of the windowpane.

Excitement flared through her, threatening to spill her magic from her grasp. She took a deep breath and centred her control.

Her fingers splayed across the glass, and with every ounce of concentration she could muster, she funnelled her magic into the window. Falling into her power, she searched for the splinter. For the pinprick that would give her more insight. A grin broke across her face as she felt the slightest resistance.

She pushed her happiness aside as she concentrated. It was difficult to break apart someone else's magic; so difficult that many never learned. Viola knew she could do it. She had broken a few of her mum's spells. But this was different. The magic seemed more complex than she had broken before.

Viola let her power wrap around the residue, searching for the thread that would allow her to pull the entire thing apart. Sweat dripped down her face. She brushed her fingers against her brow to stop the trails falling into her line of vision.

"Almost there."

The leftover pool of magic was submitting to her onslaught. Her own was frantically pulling at the strings, and she could feel the piece unravelling. She could almost see the threads pooling to the floor. Breaths came in short and sharp. Only a few pieces more remained when her energy began to falter, her magic falling from her arms.

"Not now," she whispered.

She flexed her fingers. The energy receded from her call, unwilling and reluctant to be used further. It wasn't something she had dealt with before. Whoever had placed this on the window had wanted to keep someone out. Viola squared her shoulders as the last tendrils held around the door. Her chin jutted forward. Her sleeves pushed up. Her fingers spread out as she advanced on the door. She pressed her fingers against the seams. It wasn't the most elegant way to finish the job, but elegance wasn't always the answer.

Finesse was no longer the vital part of this unravelling. Viola pushed with all her might on the threads. As much as she didn't want to go ahead with the initiation, she couldn't bear the shame of it. An Everett who hadn't been accepted into the Heather Valley coven was unheard of. She couldn't have that hanging over her head. What would her dad think if she messed this up? With that thought, she dug deeper to grasp hold of any remaining energy. Her dad's legacy wouldn't end with him.

A spark flashed through her as the last tendrils left the window. The surge pushed her to her knees. Her breath came in raggedly and uneven as she checked for remnants of the magic. Satisfied, she knocked on the door again.

"One second!" a voice trilled through the other side.

Viola pushed herself to her feet and wiped what she could of the sweat still lining her brow. The door opened. Ms. Glorian greeted her, a halo of hallway light shimmering around her. Viola shook her head to clear the imagery taking root.

"Viola, darling! We were wondering where you had gotten to. Come in from the cold." Ms. Glorian ushered her into the small house.

"Thanks," Viola said. "I would have been here sooner if I hadn't had to decipher whatever was placed on the door."

Ms. Glorian's steps faltered. "Something was on the door?"

"An added layer of protection, or a test." She let the words linger. "I had to unthread it before you could hear me."

"Of course," the older woman murmured. "Let's not keep everyone waiting."

She steered Viola into the small sitting room, the only place Ms. Glorian would allow their meetings to go ahead. At least in her house. The chatter in the room faded to nothing as she entered. Her skin prickled. A coldness seeped under her skin as she caught the eyes of Casey from the other side of the room. Disgust flashed across the other woman's face before she turned to the person next to her. Viola took a deep breath. She was doing this for her dad.

****

Viola wedged herself in a space by her mum's side. The longer she sat in the presence of the coven, the more she could feel her energy rebuilding its strength, feeding from the energies all around her. Her body sagged as she relaxed back into the feeling of safety and comfort. The man on her other side tried to make as much space for her as he could as she sank into the sofa. Ben had spoken to her a few times since she had started attending the meetings. Only witches initiated into the coven, or those intending to over the age of eighteen, were invited. She had the impression that he might have been friends with her mum and dad. If that were the case, it didn't seem as though the friendship had survived.

"I can feel the anticipation for the main event of tonight's meeting," Ms. Glorian said to the coven. Her smile was so wide, Viola was sure it was false. "However, before we begin the initiation this evening, I have a warning to issue out. Our sister coven, The High Peak, have growing concerns over the increased efforts of the hunters. With attacks across the country becoming more prolific, they have found anxiety to be running high amongst their members."

"That's impossible. Alex made sure they wouldn't be able to find us," one member of the coven spoke up.

Viola wasn't sure who they were. The man looked unfamiliar, but she caught his gaze at the mention of her dad. It wasn't often someone brought him up. Even less so to mention him by name. Whether it was from respect or shame, she couldn't be sure. No matter the reason, she had refused to mask her emotions when someone did mention him. Alex had given his life to protect the coven. No one knew if it was from the protection or if he had been taken by the witch hunters before he could return home. It was something she'd been proud of; no one else had family who had sacrificed themselves in that way. Unfortunately, it wasn't how the other children had seen it. No one wanted to be told their dad was too stupid to survive. Too stupid to avoid capture.

"Alex laid the foundation to keep us safe. Alas, that is all it was." Ms. Glorian paused as she addressed the crowd. "I know everyone here will be aware, as I, too, have heard the rumours. It is with regret that I have to inform you these are not rumours. The protection Alex gave us has slowly been wearing off. He sacrificed himself to keep us safe, but we were never able to replicate the work he had done."

Sounds of shock rippled through the crowd. The agitated energy climbed, almost reaching its crescendo when the Elder spoke again, the voice an attempt at calming the storm she had started.

"Despite the warning given to us, we are unsure of its implications within the coven. However, we are making every effort we can to keep our coven safe. The severity of this news should not be brushed aside. Each and every one of us is needed to ensure our continued survival. A twenty-year-old protection spell was never designed to keep us safe forever."

Viola watched as Ms. Glorian caught everyone's eye. The weight of her speech settled into each gathered person, their bodies tensing at the horror that could await them. Was it the light, or had Ms. Glorian's expression softened as she landed her gaze on Viola? Before she could confirm the change, the same stern look was impressed upon her as with each of the others. The apprehension had dropped within the room, but it hadn't entirely left. The threat was clear to everyone. They needed to keep the coven safe. No matter the cost.

****

"Now, onto the part everyone is excited for." Ms. Glorian beamed, her mood rapidly switching. "Today, we welcome three new initiates into the coven. We are honoured to announce these three are all of blood, and finally of age to be fully accepted into the coven. On behalf of the Elders, I would like to welcome Casey,

Viola, and William to join me. And may their magic grow and prosper for the good of the coven." She waited for the small smattering of applause to calm down before she continued. "As some of you may be aware, William joined us from High Peak not too long ago, as he moved to Sheffield to continue his studies. I hope you made him feel welcome before and are ready to welcome him fully."

With a flourish, Ms. Glorian took a step back and beckoned for Viola and the two additional initiates to take their place at the front of the gathered crowd. A small push forced Viola to take the first few steps forward. She wanted to resist, but she allowed herself to move. Turning her head slightly to the side, Viola scrunched up her face at her mum before continuing the short distance forward. Every initiate had to do this, but it wasn't something she had been looking forward to. Another chance for people to judge her without speaking to her. Casey flicked her copper hair over her shoulder as Viola joined her and William.

"We thought you'd backed out when you didn't turn up on time," she said through the side of her mouth.

"It's amazing what a bit of magic can do to keep someone out." Viola smiled sweetly at her.

"Shush." Ms. Glorian turned to them. "I know in the past we have spread these out over meetings, but due to the current situation, we have forgone our

standard practices." She turned back to the seated witches in front of her. "Everyone, please join in the welcoming. Physical contact is not necessary, but please respect your fellow witches."

Energy thrummed throughout the room at Ms. Glorian's words. The coven spread out in a haphazard semi-circle around the three, the majority holding onto one another. Viola had never been good at reading auras, but she could see them now, flashing around each person as they opened up their coven to her and the two beside her. The power held in the small room robbed Viola of her breath. Her own energy thrummed in conjunction with the room, waiting and anticipating what would be granted to them.

Ms. Glorian turned back to the three. "Now, if you could open yourselves up. To be accepted, you need to be willing to be a part of the coven. You need to give yourself freely to your brothers and sisters."

Viola nodded. She had been waiting for this moment; to prove she was a part of the coven whether they accepted her in person or not. She didn't know if she would be as successful as her dad, but she knew she would do whatever it took to follow in his footsteps. To do whatever it took to keep this coven safe.

Chapter Two

Viola breathed in the warm summer air. After the stale dirt and grime from the bus journey, she relished in the freshness of the crisp, spring afternoon. Even with the brief revival from the outside air, she had to steady herself as she made her way down the familiar path to her house. Work had been busier than usual, and with it, the use of her magic had increased. The usual hum and warmth of its presence was missing. A small voice at the back of her mind told her to hurry, but it wasn't the first time she'd over-exerted herself. She would have more than enough time.

She reached the zebra crossing. Her vision blurred. Thoughts scattered, drifting from her grasp. Her legs gave way before the world went black.

****

"…get… a hospital…" Snatched words descended on her consciousness.

Panic washed over her at the unrecognisable voice above her. As she slowly roused herself awake, she tried to remember what had happened. The thoughts came back to her in an unconnected mess, a pounding headache messing with her ability to focus on any one thought. Viola's eyes flickered open, the light from the late afternoon sun and her fringe causing a squint and a block to her vision. She used her hand to knock back the distracting strands and shield her face from the blinding light. She glanced at the man kneeling in front of her, concentrating on his face as her fuzzy vision slowly focused. There was concern written in his hazel eyes. He looked familiar; maybe he was someone who lived nearby. No matter how she looked, she couldn't place him.

Her panic had receded, but she warily pushed herself to her feet. "Wh-who are you?"

The man rose to her level, keeping his hands out in front of him. He looked pleadingly at her. "Easy there, Miss. I was trying to help." He gestured towards the car behind him. "My driver noticed you on the ground and wanted to make sure you were okay."

Viola's eyes darted over his shoulder, taking in the car and the man waiting beside it. Neither stood out at her, but she couldn't help but feel a little on edge. Ms. Glorian's warning resounded through her head. She tried flexing her energy, but it refused to respond. Damn, she felt more exposed without access to any help. She quickly dusted herself down, straightened up, and looked the man directly in the eye.

"Thanks for the help," she said, forcing her voice to remain steady, "but I'm fine. It was only a small fainting spell. Nothing a cup of tea won't fix." She grinned at him before turning to leave.

"Are you sure? We could give you a lift to wherever you were going."

"No. I'm fine, but thanks," she called back over her shoulder.

"Mr. Richardson, do you wish to continue to your destination now?" the other man, the driver, asked.

Viola stopped in her tracks before slowly turning to look at her would-be saviour. As she took in the ashy-blond hair and his square jaw, recognition hit her. With more willpower than she thought she possessed, she managed to keep her mouth firmly closed, stopping the gasp that wanted to fight its way free.

"You're David Richardson?" The words slipped from her. She wasn't able to stop all sound from leaving her.

The man, David, flashed what looked to be a confident smile at her, but it didn't reach his eyes. "The one and only, babe. Now you know my name, can I have yours?" He winked at her. Her cheeks flushed as his demeanour switched from the caring stranger he had been only a few moments before.

She laughed, light-headed and in shock. "The name's Viola." She found herself sinking into a deep curtsy. She screwed up her face while it was hidden from view. "I promise to keep your whereabouts secret if you can keep my secret?"

He raised an eyebrow. "Your secret?"

"The fainting."

"Deal," he said almost too quickly.

He held out his hand. She eyed it suspiciously, but before he could change his mind, she placed hers gently against his. Her fingers lightly squeezed his. A thrum of energy pulsed between them. She decided to look into that when her mind stopped whirring.

"I'll leave you to enjoy the rest of the city, Mr. Richardson. Try not to get hounded too much."

Before he could say anything else to her, she took off down the street and rounded into the housing estate. She made sure she was as far from the road as possible before she stopped and rested her hands on her knees. She pushed the dizziness from her mind. Home was not much further off. No need to worry about another fainting spell. The only piece of luck she had was that no one else had found her laid in a crumpled mess by the road. How long had she been out for anyway?

"Okay, at least it could have been worse," she mused, happy the only souvenir she would have would be the bump to her head.

Knowing there wasn't anything too sinister to worry about, she let a small smile flit across her face. She had met David Richardson. The David Richardson. No one would believe her if she told them. Not that she would. She'd made a deal. One she intended to keep. Still, it wasn't every day you stumbled across the most attractive businessman on TV. But that didn't mean she had to ruin whatever peace he had. No, secrets were something she traded in. Viola couldn't bring herself to speak someone else's.

****

"I'm sure I didn't leave this open," Viola muttered to herself as she entered her room.

Ebb had made use of the oversight and was lying across the bed. Her eyes lazily blinked at her owner with little sign that she would be moving from the green bedspread.

"Shoo! Come on, kitty. I need you out of here," she whispered to the feline.

Her words fell on deaf ears, or more likely the cat was ignoring her, as Ebb slowly stretched her front paws towards the corner. Viola gave her a moment to move before scooping up the tabby into her arms and depositing her into the hallway. As Viola closed the door, she heard the cat meow. Ebb would dislike the lack of attention, but she needed some time to herself, at least for now.

Viola flung her jacket onto the back of her computer chair and kicked off her scuffed trainers to rest beneath it. She walked until her calves hit the edge of her bed and fell backwards onto the comforting warmth of her mattress. She stretched out her limbs and took two deep breaths. Her mind focused on the source of her energy. It fluttered against her mental touch, but she could tell there was barely anything left. Her focus dissipated as she sat up.

"Mum is going to kill me if she finds out," Viola groaned.

She rubbed at her temples. Meditating would only help her so much. Definitely not enough for her mum to not find out about what had happened. But what choice did she have? At least with this, it would cover up the worst of it.

"No time like the present." She flicked her hand to close the blinds with the last of her remaining energy.

She scooted into the middle of the bed and let her

arms and legs cover as much of the space as they could before she started to fall into a more comfortable position. Her eyes fell closed as the energy inside her began to hum. It fluttered against her, fanning out across her torso and down her legs. She relaxed into the feeling, giving it more reign. The hum deepened, vibrations joining the flutters over her body. The vibrations continued until the sensation made her stomach churn. Even with her eyes closed, the room moved around her. Her thoughts swam and lost themselves into the feelings. She knew she wouldn't be able to sit for much longer. It wouldn't be enough time to fully refresh the energy, but at least it wouldn't feed from her consciousness.

Her eyes drifted open and she concentrated on the ceiling as her vision began to clear. Her mind was distracted by the shimmering of the aura still dancing on her arms. The room stopped spinning, and the nausea receded. Hopefully, that would be the last of the fainting spells she would have for a long while. Her legs ached from the crossed position she had pulled herself into. A few short steps to the window and the ache in her legs dulled. She yanked on the chain and the blinds no longer blanketed the room from the mid-afternoon light. The darkness wasn't necessary for the meditation to work, but it was necessary to hide the kaleidoscope of colours that danced around her during such a session.

Viola glanced at her arms again. There was always a small sense of disappointment once the colours receded. They might have been a tell-tale sign she wasn't 100% human, but they were a reminder of how nature could be unpredictable. Auras weren't always visible to non-witches, but it was better to be safe than burned at the stake. With the increased worry within the coven, she didn't want to do anything that might cause future issues. The witch trials weren't as prolific as they had been. It didn't mean she wanted to test it.

The only safe way to survive was to stay hidden. When your enemy was also driven underground, it was easier to get caught. The threat was always lurking in the shadows, more sinister than a bogeyman hiding under a bed. With the legacy she had to grow into, she had tried to reduce the risks.

****

Viola didn't know how long she had been lying on her bed when the scratches started at her door. Ebb continued the activity until she let the cat back into her room.

"You're being patient as ever," Viola said.

As soon as the door opened, the cat darted into the room and made her way to the sun spot, which had moved to the corner of the bed.

"I missed you, too," she said as she clambered back onto her bed and curled around the cat.

She scratched the back of Ebb's ears and was gifted with a low, rumbled purr. Viola let her hand drift back to the mattress. She sighed and disrupted the peace as she swept the cat into her arms.

"C'mon, let's grab you some food."

"You shouldn't carry her like that. She'll get lazy," Emilia called as Viola walked into the kitchen.

"Mum! When did you get home? I didn't hear you come in."

"I'm not surprised with how long you've been building up your energy." Emilia turned to face her daughter, still peeling the potato in her hand. "Want to tell me why something like that was needed?" She raised her eyebrow.

"It's not a big deal, Mum. I might have pushed myself a little harder than I intended to at work, and I didn't factor in the initiation change as well. It's not as bad as it looks, though. I fainted for a few minutes, but I got home without issue." Viola clapped a hand over her mouth. "I hate it when you do that."

"Sometimes you need a little push to tell the full truth." Emilia pinched the bridge of nose. "People told me not to let you become a nurse, Viola. It was all; *Emilia this is a bad idea. Emilia, she will get us all found out. Emilia, you can't control your daughter.*" Viola squirmed under her gaze. "I'm starting to think they were right." Despite her words, Emilia smiled at Viola. "I am very proud of you, despite the complaints I receive. I wish you would take more care of yourself."

"I'm sorry. I know I should have rested better before work and maybe listened to myself more. But, I have to help people. It's not fair to be blessed with something like this." She gestured wildly around herself, "and not use it to help. To help everyone. Even those outside of the coven. I want to do more than I am, but the small handful that I am helping is more than enough for now."

Emilia put down her cooking and pulled Viola into a hug. "I know, I know. It's why I love you even when you're giving me grey hairs. Remember, you can't help if you don't help yourself. Could you try to be a little more cautious in future?"

Viola disentangled herself from her mum's arm. "I can promise to try."

Emilia chuckled. "Your father would be proud of you. But maybe a little more than try. We don't want to see the whole coven wiped out, do we?"

Viola shook her head.

"Okay, now the parenting is out of the way, you can help with the rest of this cooking," Emilia said as she went back to her previous ministrations.

Chapter Three

"Viola, please can you pull the chairs from the cupboard?" Emilia called from the kitchen.

"Yes, Mum."

The small living room was overcrowded with seating places. The house wasn't big to begin with, though it was perfect for two witches who enjoyed spending time with each other. But the entire coven? It was going to be a cramped few hours. Maybe there was a way to make the room seem bigger, or at least a way to alter the space in the room.

"Don't even think about it." The sentence caused Viola to jump.

"What do you mean?"

"I can see the way you're eyeing up this room. I am not having you mess with the space and not be able to get it back to normal. How would we explain it? Hmm?"

"It wouldn't be that noticeable."

"How do you know?"

Viola sighed. "I don't, but it's not like it's a difficult use of energy. I know I could do it."

"Viola, we can cope without the extra space. They've had to cope before, and they'll cope again tonight. The chairs can go over there."

"Fine, I'll leave it the way it is. But I'll find a way to push it out one day without you realising."

"There's nothing I won't realise in this house." Emilia's voice drifted away as she left the room.

Viola pushed the coffee table out of the way to make room for all the fold-up chairs. They should be able to comfortably fit the expected thirty people. As long as the meeting didn't overrun, like usual, it shouldn't be much of a problem. She could always perch on top of the table if they were too sardined into the space. She eyed the table before jumping on top of it. If it was going to collapse, she'd rather it was before anyone else turned up.

Satisfied with the work she'd done, she checked her mum couldn't see her and pushed her energy around the room. It wasn't always easy to manipulate space, but she had been working on noise cancelling in her own bedroom. Not that she thought there would be anyone trying to eavesdrop on the meeting. It never hurt to be cautious. Now, whatever they spoke about wouldn't be overheard even if someone was trying. The thought of the coven being exposed had pushed Viola to work harder. As she finished her task, the lull of her energy softened.

She propped herself up on unsteady legs. "Mum?"

No response. She grinned. One less thing to worry about this evening. Now all that was left to discover was the need for such an urgent meeting.

****

The noise in the room thrummed, expectant murmurs and conjectures whispered among friends. Viola perched herself on the table pushed into the corner. As William made his way into the room, he looked over at her and caught her eye. When she noticed him, he smiled at her. She smiled nervously back. What did he want? He'd never had any contact with her before.

Her eyes scanned over everyone gathered there. The coven was her family; she would do anything to keep them safe, but she didn't count them as friends. Maybe at one point, she was closer to the ones her age, but that hadn't been the case for most of what she remembered. As they aged, the distance between them grew. Viola continued her regular magic use and helped whoever she could. They weren't willing to help anyone. It confused and upset her. As soon as she realised they wouldn't help, she found herself drifting away from her friends. Now, they were the distant cousins she didn't want to see get hurt.

"I'm sure you are wondering why I have convened us all here tonight," Ms. Glorian spoke, breaking Viola from her thoughts. "I want to say thank you to Emilia and Viola for being able to host us with such short notice."

"It's an honour to have everyone here," Emilia responded.

Viola kept quiet.

"I'm sure," Ms. Glorian said. "We have had had some distressing news from the High Peak Coven today. One of theirs has disappeared, a young woman by the name of Sophie. No one knows where she has gone, and she has not responded to any of the usual contact methods. They will be following the necessary procedures and protocols, but they needed to warn us in case it was something more sinister."

"More sinister?" William asked.

Viola's eyebrows shot up. No one ever interrupted Ms. Glorian at an emergency meeting. Especially not a new initiate. The situation must have been more troubling than the Elder was letting on if she had ignored it.

"We all know the protection magic is wearing off. They believe theirs has failed, which has allowed a witch hunter to find them. It is a serious worry, and even more reason why we need to pool our strength to keep safe." She looked around the cramped group. When she moved her gaze to Viola, Viola made sure to hold it. And also her tongue. "I know we have been reserved in our magic workings over the years, and we still need to be cautious. However, it is now imperative we do everything we can to keep our families safe. As of today, we all need to include a small daily practice into our lives."

"Alex would never have let this happen. He gave himself up for this coven, and this is the message you give us," a man from the front said. Viola couldn't place him.

"Thomas, that is enough. You know how we tried to save Alex."

"He didn't need saving; he needed your help."

Ms. Glorian sighed. "We will not be having this discussion again. And not in public." She turned her attention back to everyone in the room. "I know this will be a change, but myself and the other Elders are here to help you."

"How will we do that?"

"Won't we be caught if we're practising too much?"

"What if we can't practice?"

"Will the witch hunters really find us?"

The cacophony of questions sounded out and overlapped. The energy frayed over them, pushing their anxiety to higher levels as each new question reached their ears and compounded their fears. Viola wished she had protected her corner of the room from loud noises and the agitated feeling of their collective energy.

"Enough." Emilia's sharp voice reverberated around the assembled witches. "This will not help us keep our families or our friends safe. Ms. Glorian has asked us to practice, so we must practice. If anyone needs help in finding basic techniques to try, I will be more than happy to sit with them. We *will* keep our coven safe."

An almost deathly silence wrapped around the witches. The buzz of the energy quietened to a manageable hum. Pride swelled through Viola's body. Her mum did not usually speak out during the meetings, but these were not normal circumstances. Emilia had returned to her seat, waiting for the meeting to run its course.

"Thank you, Emilia." Ms. Glorian smiled graciously at her. "We will do as Mrs. Everett said. We will keep this coven safe, and with the warning from our brothers and sisters to the West, we will have the time to do this. If any of you would like to discuss this further, we can do this in private when we can hear each other rather than shouting and screaming like a bunch of school children. However, before we go our own ways, I think it is pertinent to note there was a warning left close to the missing girl's home. From this, we know it was a targeted attack on this young woman, but we have not been given any details as to what was written on the note. I want you all to be extra careful when you begin your daily practice. This is not the time to be trying to be the hero or heroine." Her eyes again carefully met everyone's in the room. The weight of her words settled heavily on the assembled crowd.

"Who would like a drink?" Emilia asked, trying to lighten the now dour mood.

As people began to move around the downstairs of the house, Viola stayed where she was, thinking over the warning. As she mulled over the varying thoughts, she noticed someone standing in front of her.

"You really that worried?"

Viola looked up to see William peering at her.

"Aren't you?" she shot back.

"Yeah." His eyes went distant. "I don't like it. But that's why I'm here. I've heard you have never taken the rules seriously and you might be one of the most powerful witches we have."

"I don't believe that," Viola scoffed.

"I don't know many others who use their magic as freely as you do. I wouldn't be surprised if you're the only one who uses it daily as it is. Everyone talks about it."

"They do?" Viola knew some gossip circulated about her, but she didn't know that was something they all talked about.

"Don't worry, it's not all the time," William added hastily. "But I think you might be the best hope we have."

"Thanks, but not to be rude, I don't think you should all be pinning your hopes on me. I'm not my dad. I can't do what he did. I don't know what he did. So, if that's the only reasons you're talking to me, then maybe don't." With that, she slid from the table and went to search for her mum.

William reached out to her before she could get past him. "Please."

The word halted her advance.

"Sophie was a good friend of mine. We hadn't spoken as much as we used to, but I tried to contact her a few days ago and heard nothing. I thought something was wrong but didn't think to mention it."

Viola paused, his earlier outburst making more sense. "Look, I would love to do something to help but I don't think I'm that person. I use my power to help where I can, but I've never looked into how my dad was able to put the protection in place, or how he did anything. I know everyone thinks he was this amazingly powerful witch, but I've never said I want to be like him. Sorry, William, but I don't think I'm the person you're looking for."

William nodded at her. She pulled her arm from his grasp. She didn't need any more pressure to live up to her dad's legacy.

****

The serenity of the room relaxed her after the chatter of the coven all evening. Viola had wanted to head to bed long before everyone had gone home, but she had been told in no uncertain terms she was to socialise until every last guest had left. It was the first time in a long while since they had hosted the coven meeting, and she had forgotten how tiring playing hostess could be. The questions from the crowd hadn't dissipated, they had only quietened and become more targeted after her mum's mini speech.

"Do you think we need to worry?" Viola asked her mum as they tidied.

"I think it would be wise to be more careful," Emilia said, weighing her choice of words. "If there was a note or warning left near the home, this was targeted, and we are slowly losing the protection we've enjoyed."

"We'll be able to get it back, though, right? Dad let people know how to keep it going?"

"I hope so, but he never left anything with him. It has been nice without the worry and fear, though."

"Was it that bad before?" Viola murmured.

Emilia's eyes flickered with fear. Viola could read it with her own energy before her mum regained her composure. "It was difficult. Not as difficult as it used to be, but you didn't know who you could trust. There were more people disappearing than there are now. If we can't find a way to strengthen the protections, we may face the same problem again."

Viola's skin prickled at the potential future. "I'm sure it won't come to that."

Emilia smiled weakly. "If we work together, then maybe." She glanced at the wall as she folded the last chair. Her eyes flickered to the wall. "You should get off. Don't you have an early shift tomorrow?"

Viola groaned as her gaze followed her mum's. The time on the clock stared down at her. It was almost midnight. "Eurgh, I'll never get any sleep before work now."

She trudged to her room and flopped onto the bed, too tired to take off her clothes. It would be easier for her to leave in the morning if she kept them on.

William's words swirled around her mind. There had to be a way they could keep safe. A way they could stop the protection being lifted completely. It was ridiculous to think a full group of people wouldn't be able to achieve what her dad had. Annoyance bubbled through her, and she knew she would need to focus on something else if she had any hope of getting some sleep.

She tossed and turned in bed as she tried to force herself to sleep. None came, but her thoughts drifted to her strange encounter and the reaction her energy had to David Richardson's touch. Despite being found in a crumpled heap by the road, she couldn't help but wonder why he'd stopped to help. He couldn't have much free time to himself. Not that he had done much in the end.

Still, her mind churned over the events. She couldn't figure out how he'd managed to revive her so easily. Was that part of the energy reaction? She'd only ever passed out from the over-use once before. Luckily, she had been at home, but she had been out for hours that time. It couldn't have been more than thirty minutes when he happened by her. She wanted to ask someone about it, to see what could have caused the almost instant revival. Not that she would be asking her mum any time soon. That was not a conversation she wanted to go into much detail with. Maybe she could ask her about the energy in a more roundabout way.

She nestled herself under the duvet cover, sinking into her pillows and letting the bed envelop her into a dream-like state. Maybe she could find her mum's books and see if there was anything there. Probably not, but it would be a good place to start.

Chapter Four

nother day finished at the hospital, and another day when the main bus home was running late. Or, as Viola believed, was refusing to go to the stop she waited at. She looked across the road before making her way towards the bus station. It would make her journey a little longer, but at least she knew she'd be able to make it home without any issues. Viola had zoned in on her goal of reaching her destination, so she didn't notice the person jogging to her left until they collided with her

The air tore from her lungs as she fell to the floor. Her earlier mood did not help how she felt, but before she could say anything, her assailant spoke.

"Shit, I'm sorry. I didn't see anyone," the man started to explain but stopped. "It's you."

Viola dusted herself down but tried to hide her own amazement as she pulled herself to her feet. She barely recognised him under the giant cap and sunglasses. "We need to stop running into each other like this."

"Are you okay? I've not sprained anything, have I?" David asked, his words rushing from his mouth as his eyes looked over her.

"No, no. I'll be fine. Maybe a bruised coccyx, but nothing to worry about." She took a step back. "I'll let you get back to wherever you were running off to." She smiled at him. "Although, I'd try to be more aware. You don't want to end up in hospital on your trip."

"It looks like it's you who's more likely to be in the hospital."

"Only one of the two times you've seen me on the floor has been caused by me."

"Touché." David ran his hand through his hair. "I was about to head out into the country for a bit, to escape from all this." He gestured behind him. "Would you like to come with me?" He looked surprised at his own question.

"What?"

"Erm, would you like to come with me?" he asked again. He sounded less sure than he had a second ago.

Viola stared at him. Had she hit her head when she'd fallen? This had to be some sort of joke, but she wasn't sure how.

"It sounds like you want some time to yourself. You don't have to take pity on me and ruin that. I forgive you for running into me." She forced herself to smile.

She watched as his face dropped slightly before he recovered. "It would be nice to have some company, but I get it. You don't know me, and a trip into the country with a man you've only recently met is maybe not the best idea." He paused before looking around himself. "Maybe I'll run into you again sometime."

As he turned to leave, Viola felt the urge to stop him. "Wait." He turned as she called him. "Give me your phone. If you ever feel like a non-creepy way to spend time with people, drop me a message." David handed over his phone as Viola entered her own number into it. "But I can't say I'll always respond." She smiled at him as she handed it back.

"How about a coffee?"

"Weren't you heading out of the city?"

"I might have changed my mind on how I want to escape."

"Coffee sounds less creepy."

****

"What brings you to Sheffield?" Viola asked as she sipped at the still-hot coffee. She sank into the oversized chair, relishing the weight off her feet. The dimmed lighting and hushed music pulled her into a relaxed state.

"Who are you? An undercover journalist?" David laughed at her, resting his sunglasses by his cup.

"No, just curious. It's not that often you bump into the same famous person for the second time in as many weeks."

David stared at her. Viola fidgeted under the intensity of it. "I'm visiting family," he said eventually.

"Oh, you grew up around here?"

"Not in the centre, but Sheffield was where I made my start."

"Now I feel like an idiot."

"Why?" David asked, his eyebrows furrowed.

"Telling you to enjoy the city and the curtsy."

"It was cute." He laughed. "It made a lasting impression."

Viola groaned into her hand. "I'm not sure that's the impression I would want to give. My only saving grace is I had just woken from a fainting episode." She threw a scrunched-up napkin at him. "You can stop laughing at me now."

"I'll try," he said, but Viola could still see the laughter in his eyes.

"Sure, sure. I believe you one hundred percent."

"So, from that, I guess you never read the biography?"

Viola laughed, twisting the fallen strands of hair to rest behind her ear. "No, never read the book." She paused, toying with her question. "Did you ever think it would get as bad as it has? The fame and being recognised," she added at his blank look.

"I didn't think about it at all. I was in business, not normally the most famous of job roles. I thought it would be a quiet show only watched by a handful of people. I guess I should have realised how intrusive reality TV was." He smiled wryly. "Not that I can make any changes to that now."

"Are the investments you make real? It's not all show for the cameras, you want to help them?"

"Yeah, if the owners let me. They don't always appreciate the way I've infiltrated the lower levels. I can't argue with them as it would annoy me if anyone did it to my company. It's the ones I don't want to invest in that can become more of a hassle. A lot of the ending for that isn't shown." He took a small drink of his tea.

Viola paused. "Have you ever thought of stopping it?"

"Contracts. I have to do two more seasons before I can renegotiate. Who knows what will happen after that."

"I feel like I'm being given insider knowledge," Viola said, her eyes twinkling mischievously.

"What's your silence worth?"

She tapped her chin. "Hmm, at least another coffee."

David grinned at her. "I'm sure that can be arranged."

"I feel like I've sold myself short. Maybe I should have gone for something slightly more valuable."

"Like dinner?"

Viola tried to calm the racing of her heart at his words. She tried to skim past it. "I was thinking something more extreme. Maybe a flying lesson."

"A flying lesson? I didn't see you as the type."

"You caught me. I couldn't think of anything more extreme."

They sat in comfortable silence as the conversation lapsed. Viola savoured the last of her coffee and checked the time.

"I'm sorry, I'm going to have to go. My family will be worried about where I am." She gathered up her few belongings and stood from the table. "Thank you for the coffee and the insider scoop. I hope you have a great time with your family."

David followed her movements, and before she could leave the table, he reached across and let his fingers graze against her wrist. Her energy lurched against the feeling. "Don't feel like you have to rush off straight away. I could get you a ride home if you want."

"No, I wouldn't want to put anyone out." She pulled her arm from his touch. She resisted the urge to run her fingers along her forearm. "If you have any more breaking news stories, let me know and I'll meet you for that other coffee."

"Or dinner." A smile broke out across his features.

****

Viola walked down the path to her house with a ridiculous smile plastered across her face. One that had refused to leave since she had taken her leave from the café. Her stomach fluttered. She didn't feel twenty-five anymore, but more like a teenager with their first crush.

"Calm down, girl. Stop getting your head in a spin."

"Viola!" a voice shouted to her as she reached her garden gate.

She turned to see William coming towards her. She rolled her eyes. How many times would she have to tell him she didn't want to help him with whatever he was planning?

"What do you want?" she asked, trying and failing to keep the annoyance from her voice.

William paid no attention to her tone, or at least he didn't let it affect him. "I want to talk. Your mum said I should try that rather than pouncing on you like the other day at the meeting. Sorry, I was carried away with my own ideas."

"Fine. If my mum has her fingers in it, I guess I should at least hear you out. Do you want to come inside?" She stood with the gate open for him.

"Sure." He smiled as he walked towards the front

door.

Once they were settled in the kitchen, she made sure the room was secure. Her eyes closed as she let the magic soundproof the room. As she turned to look at William, he stared with his mouth hanging wide open.

"What?"

"Nothing, nothing. I mean…" He rubbed his chin. "I've never seen anyone else perform magic so easily before. Are you sure you aren't the strongest member of this coven? Or any coven."

Viola glared at him.

"Okay, okay," he said, chuckling nervously. "Look, I know you might not think you can help, but I'd appreciate it if you could help me with my daily practice. I know you use your magic, and from what I saw, I think you are the best choice." He shifted in his seat. "Can I speak openly here?"

"What do you think I was doing?" Viola asked him. He stared blankly at her. "The room is soundproofed, at least for the time being. Feel free to say what you want."

William caught himself as his mouth began to drop open. "Right, okay. I want to find out about the protection spell your dad created. I thought with us being the newest initiates, and it being your dad, we might be able to work through something together. We know he was one of the strongest we've had, but no one will say anything about what he did. If we worked together, we might be able to come up with it or find something that points us in the right direction."

"Look, William," Viola started, "I wish I could help, I really do, but I already told you that I have no idea what magic he did. Or how we could replicate it. I don't know where the magic was performed, so I can't even go and feel it out for myself. If I knew what it was, I'd already be trying to do something to help, especially now."

"Feel it out…" William began speaking, his voice trailing off as the words settled over him. "That would be helpful. Didn't he leave behind any grimoires or books we could go through?"

"Maybe. I don't know." She shrugged, pushing the thought to the back of her mind. "I've never thought to ask about any grimoires, or if he'd recorded any of his practising."

"Will you ask?"

"I guess there's no harm in it," she conceded.

"Perfect, and the practice?"

"If you want to practise, I can't show you." She paused. "If you want to get better, you need to start doing small things. Opening curtains, turning off lights, moving coats. That sort of thing. Once you can do these every day and don't feel a strain on your magic, you can move on to my difficult things. I can't show you anything advanced until I know you'll be okay to learn it.

One thing I would say would be to keep your practice confined to the house and don't push yourself too hard. Use too much at once or don't give enough time to recharge and you might collapse."

"Collapse?"

"Occupational hazard."

"Thanks, Viola. This is more than anyone else has done." He stood from the chair. "But the other thing? You'll help?"

"I want nothing more than to keep this coven safe,

but we don't have any idea of what we need to do to get there. So, no. I don't want to waste my time on something I don't think will work."

William pulled a face at her. Before he or Viola could say anything, he grabbed a scrap of paper from the edge of the kitchen table and pulled a pen from his pocket.

"In case you change your mind." He smiled and passed the note across to her. "I won't bother you any more tonight."

He left Viola to read his scrawling. It was a phone number.

"I don't think I'll be needing that any time soon," she said as she stuffed the paper into the kitchen drawer.

Chapter Five

"I need his books, or whatever he left behind." Viola confronted her mum as soon as she entered the house. William's words had been playing on her mind. Why didn't she know where any of her dad's stuff was? And why was no one else trying to look for them?

"What would you need those for?" Emilia asked, her hand resting dangerously on her hip.

Viola sighed and stood up from her rooting through the bookshelf. "If Dad was the only person who knew how to do the protection spell, wouldn't he have made sure to note it down, or leave some information for someone else to be able to help out?"

"You think he knew he wouldn't be here to help?" Her eyebrow raised.

Viola paused. "No, I don't think that," she started slowly. "But aren't we all supposed to record what we're doing? Especially new magic, so that we can use it for our records later on? Please, Mum. I want to be able to help the coven."

"I'm not talking to you about this," Emilia said, starting to turn away.

"Please. If I only had his books, I might be able to keep us all safe." Viola grasped at her arm.

"I said I'm not talking to you about this right now." Her voice trembled with pain and grief.

"I want to help." Viola couldn't stop the sound of tears clogging up her voice.

"I know you do," Emilia said, gently squeezing Viola's hand. "You always want to help. But maybe I don't want to worry about losing you, too. Please, Viola. Don't ask me to find his things. I don't know if I could bear it."

"Okay." Viola fiddled with a piece of hair that had escaped from her bun. "I'll see you in the morning?"

"Maybe, sweetheart. I don't know if I'll be gone before you need to wake up."

Viola placed the piles of books back onto the shelf before making her way upstairs, keeping one of them tucked under her arm. She wasn't deterred by her mum's refusal. If anything, it meant something had been left behind. William was right. It left a sour taste in her mouth.

How long had she been using her magic without thinking about the protection spell? She could have been spending more of her life looking into it and what it needed to keep its power going. She changed into her pyjamas when she entered her room. There was no guarantee she would have been able to figure it out without her dad's writings, but now she needed them. They all needed them. She curled herself around Ebb's sleeping form on the bed and placed the book on the pillow next to her.

A thought came to her. If she found something in the house he'd touched, something he'd used magic on, she might be able to pick on his signature. It was a long shot, but it might be the only way to find his books without her mum's help.

Would power linger after twenty years? Sure, the protection was still in place, but that would have been more complex. Would it be possible for a small trace to be waiting for her to pick it apart? It didn't matter that the odds were stacked against her. Ms. Glorian was right; everyone needed to do what they could to keep the coven safe.

With her mind made up, Viola sprang from the bed in search of her own notebook. She flicked through the pages until she came to something she had recently started working through. The pages lay open on her desk as she sank into the chair. She let her magic rise up until she could feel the vibrations along her skin. A couple of breaths focused her mind, and she pushed the energy out, expanding it to fill the room. She gently brushed her magic across every surface and object it came against, feeling for any left-behind magic. She could feel the leftovers from her own practice earlier, but it was faint. Weak.

She scrunched up her face as she pushed the energy towards the door and along the hallway. She tried to picture the house in her mind as she let her magic flow from her. The further she pushed, the less she was able to feel. Annoyance flashed through her, and her control slipped.

Frustrated, she flung herself back onto the bed.

"Just once, Ebb. Just once I'd like things to be easy."

The cat only purred in response.

If she couldn't find anything in the house to help her, she was going to have to search for her dad's things. It wasn't going to be an easy task. If her mum had hidden them, they would be somewhere no one would be able to find with magic. It would be the only safe way to keep them hidden from anyone else in the coven. But this was her mum. Surely, she knew where all the hiding spots were in the house? Although, now she thought about, she'd never been able to find her birthday or Christmas presents growing up. It might be harder than she thought.

Viola tossed and turned in bed, Ms. Glorian's words echoing in the back of her mind. If the key to finding out what her dad had been working on was through the unravelling of his work, maybe she could do it. It would be difficult on her own, but that wouldn't stop her. The coven needed her, and she wasn't about to let them down. Viola let herself drift off. A good night's rest might be what she needed to work out her current predicament.

****

Viola woke with a start.

She checked her phone, and only four hours had passed since she fell asleep. She sighed and pushed herself up. Ebb moved closer to her, nudging her arm.

"What's up?" Viola asked as she ran her fingers across the cat's head.

Ebb nudged at her arm again.

Viola looked to her side and remembered the

discarded notebook.

"Thanks," she said as she flicked through the pages. Viola scanned each page, looking for anything on regeneration or energy reaction. She found nothing on the former, but there was one line that looked useful.

'When we find someone equally blessed, our energies will rush to meet them.'

She read over the line a few times. It wasn't something she'd heard mentioned within the coven, and this was from one of her mum's own books. Could it be that there was a way for her energy to react to someone? It would explain the strange surges when she had been near David, but it didn't make any sense. She tried to think of any other time she had felt such a shock when she touched anyone. There wasn't a single instance when it had happened to her before.

The line sat in her mind almost as if it wanted Viola to understand it. What did her mum mean by equally blessed? Her fingers itched to highlight the line and jot down anything that she could think of, but her mum would not appreciate the annotations to her records. She tapped her fingers on her cheek. Could it mean David had access to magic as well? It wasn't unheard of to have unregistered witches born, but the covens had abided by strict rules since the burnings.

There should be some record of his family line somewhere, even if he hadn't been directly registered. She slumped back into the pillow and rested her head on her knees. She sighed, there wasn't a single person she could trust to ask about this information. It would cause too many questions over something she had no proof of.

She tried to think if this had happened to her

before. If it was only a way to determine if another person was a witch, surely it was something everyone would experience when in contact with the coven. But she couldn't think of a single time this might have happened before. With her fingers holding the pages open, she took a picture so she could remember what this said when she had more time to research it.

Chapter Six

The sun wasn't out, which was to be expected in April, but at least it wasn't raining. The Peak District would be the perfect place to get out and use her magic without anyone seeing. With the weather being a little worse than pleasant, Viola was hoping it would put off even more people from taking a hike.

She didn't come out here often to practise, but the solitude helped clear her mind. There was no bustling of the road nearby, or the sounds of the neighbours walking and moving around next door. Here, she could find a spot and sit in peace.

She'd woken with the need to practise. To strengthen her magic. To keep everyone safe. Viola decided her day off would be put to the good of the coven. Hopefully, her plan would push her magic to the next level.

She pulled herself through the heather and over the

rocks to find somewhere sheltered. Somewhere away from the more used areas. She found a spot hidden by the half-built walls and pulled the blanket from her rucksack. It landed haphazardly on the ground. Viola straightened out the edge closest to her before sinking to the floor. She laid her bag by her side and closed her eyes for a few moments.

"Yep, this will do," she said to herself.

Her hands grasped the cold, sharp porcelain from her bag. She placed the broken mug on the blanket in front of her. She didn't know if distance would matter, but she didn't want to tempt anything by spreading the broken pieces across the entire fabric.

Viola stretched herself out, loosening up her limbs and letting her energy engulf her. She opened her mind and her senses, allowing her consciousness to brush against her energy. Her body tingled in response. She allowed her breaths to even out. Her chest steadily rose and fell as she relaxed into the feeling. She'd had a theory for a while, one that she hadn't wanted to speak out loud.

She meditated, as she did whenever her energy was low, and concentrated on how she felt. The humming began to tingle down her arms and legs, but instead of falling into the sensation as she usually did, she opened her eyes. The broken pieces of the mug captured her full attention. In her mind, she saw them as one, joined completely. She directed the humming on the mug like she would the fluttering feeling of her energy.

This was more unwieldy. Where her energy could be manipulated and pushed as though wafting a butterfly, this pulled and turned, writhing like a snake. Her tongue jutted out of the corner of her mouth as she attempted to keep it under control. It wouldn't listen to her prodding or poking, and the humming slipped from her mind's grasp and continued to overtake her body.

She pulled herself from the feeling, from the meditation. Jumping to her feet, she shook the remaining tingles from her body. The tell-tale aura of her meditating still emanated faintly from her skin, but she didn't have time to worry about that.

"C'mon, Viola. You can do this. You almost had it." She psyched herself up.

She wanted to continue, but her body felt restless. Too much energy was pent up inside. She bounced lightly on her toes, stretching her arms out above her head. It might not have done much, but it calmed her enough to fold back onto the blanket with her legs crossed beneath her. Her brow scrunched, and her mouth puckered as the humming returned to her limbs. As soon as she felt the sensation through her body, she grasped it and focused all her attention on the mug.

The feeling fought against her, straining and pushing back from where she directed it. But this time, she could feel it moving in the right direction. It felt almost as difficult as unravelling the magic left on the door. Sweat beaded on her face. The more she concentrated, the more she could feel it listening to her. She tried not to let the shock of it working get the better of her.

Viola watched as it slowly began to repair itself. The pieces in front of her slowly fused together. She waited until she was sure her plan had worked before allowing the humming to flow from her grasp. Her fingers ran over the now smooth piece of crockery, eyes wide that it had worked. Viola couldn't stop the grin that slowly spread across her face, lighting up every part of it. If she could find a way to control this instead of the energy inside her then she might be able to finish what her dad started. With or without his notes.

The use of energy that wasn't her own had made her head spin. She wouldn't let this minor drawback ruin her mood. Her heart raced, and the smile stretching across her face almost hurt. She'd done it. From all her readings, she had never seen anyone attempt this. Or, if they had, they hadn't recorded it. This could change everything for the coven. If only she knew of a way to broach the subject. How could she tell them the type of magic she had been working on? She pulled her phone from her pocket and added her experiment and findings to her notes app. It might not be a typical grimoire, but it worked on the go.

Chapter Seven

Viola sat at the computer station. There were only a few minutes left of her shift, and she hoped to leave before they asked her to stay any longer. She didn't usually mind, but she could feel how tired she was. She didn't usually push her magic so hard, but she was practising every chance she got on top of how much she usually used.

"Where's your head at?" Rachel asked her as she dropped her files onto the space beside her.

"Uh, what?"

"You're really not with it today."

"Sorry. It's been one of those days." Viola yawned, stretching out her arms. "Plus, admin has always been the bit I've disliked."

Rachel laughed. "Who wants to be doing admin when they can help people?"

"I swear they only made us do this to drive us insane. It should be banned under the Geneva

Convention." Viola leaned back in her chair. "They are making us do more, right? It feels like I've always got more and more notes to fill out."

"Maybe. Or maybe you just don't get yours done on time."

"I don't know what you're talking about." She couldn't help the grin from taking over and lifting her mood.

"There's the Viola we normally see." Rachel sat at the desk next to her. "What's the plan for clocking off? A wonderful night filled with pizza and reality TV?"

"I wish! If I'm lucky, I will sleep until I need to be here tomorrow."

"Aren't you off tomorrow?"

"I'm supposed to be, but you know what it's like. They always need someone extra in."

"Vi, you need to take the time off. Just because you don't have kids, or a fella, doesn't mean you should be spending all your time here. I'm going to tell them you're busy. Enjoy your day off. Speaking of…" Rachel looked at her watch. "I think that's you done."

"Fine. I might use tomorrow to sleep all day instead. I don't need two mums, you know," Viola said, sticking her tongue out at her friend.

"Whatever. See you in a few days."

Viola quickly switched from her nurse's scrubs to her travel clothes. If she was lucky, she'd be able to make the next bus. As she hurried through the car park to the main road, her phone buzzed in her hand. She looked at the notification to see a text from an unknown number. She almost ignored it, but her eyes skimmed the first few words.

Hey, I know it's been a couple of weeks. I've not been able to get in touch before, but I was hoping you would be up for making that journey into the Peak District. The weather's meant to be nice this evening. And I can bring a picnic. D x

Viola scrunched up her face. Who would want to take her out at such short notice? Who was D? She started typing out a wrong number reply when the realisation hit her like a soaring rock to the face. David.

Right now? I'm not sure I'm dressed for the hills, but a picnic sounds fun. Where should I meet you? X

She was glad she'd changed from her work clothes.

Where are you? I'll pick you up x

****

"I miss being able to come here whenever I want," David said as they walked up the hill.

"What do you mean?" Viola asked, struggling to follow the path he'd taken.

David turned to smile at her. "This was one of my favourite places growing up. My friends and I built a den over there when we were around fourteen, maybe fifteen. I didn't realise I wouldn't have the chance to spend time out here when I grew up. Nowhere else feels like it does here."

"You could be anywhere in the world, and this is the best place?" Viola shook her head. "I can't believe there aren't other places that offer the same as this."

David nodded. "You'd think so, but there's

something about the hills and the feeling of peace I've never found anywhere else. Whenever I step out here, I can feel all my stress leaving my body. I feel recharged."

"I guess you don't appreciate something until you can't have it."

"Something like that." The words were almost lost in the wind.

Viola blushed under his gaze. She cleared her throat. "So, where's the den?"

He turned from her, taking in the countryside. Small wrinkles appeared at the corners of his eyes. Viola couldn't help but stare at him when he wasn't facing her.

"Okay, it's in this sort of direction," he said as he started walking.

"Sort of direction? That's not filling me with a lot of hope," Viola shouted at his moving form.

They walked along a gravel path as it veered further into the hills. She followed as David took a side trail away from the main path, down towards the river. It didn't look as well-worn, and Viola jogged to keep up with him. A few times he turned to check on her. Whenever she caught his gaze, she'd flash him a smile and give him a thumbs up.

He led them to a point where the river almost seemed to struggle against the bed. It wasn't fast-flowing, but Viola thought it looked cold. All water looked cold and unappealing to her. David turned back to face her. Viola shifted slightly as he stared at her legs.

"Face is up here, David."

He had the grace to blush. "I was checking how tall you are."

"Uh-huh."

"No, really. I wanted to make sure you could cross without ruining your shoes. I didn't exactly warn you about the river."

Her eyes glanced towards the gurgling water below the banking. She pushed her shoulders back and bit on the corner of her lip as she sized up the path in front of them.

"I can manage it."

"You sure your shoes will be okay?"

"I only wear them to and from work. I can find another pair if these get too wet. Plus, if they get ruined, I'm sure a gentleman would replace them."

"Is that the only reason you came?"

Viola jumped at the bitterness in his voice. Harsh and without warning. "To have my shoes ruined?" A small crease appeared on her brows. "Definitely. I couldn't think of a better way to spend my Thursday evening."

"Sorry." He refused to meet her eyes. "I shouldn't have snapped like that."

"As long as you keep the snappiness to a minimum, we'll be good."

David turned from her. The sour feeling surrounding them disappeared almost as soon as it had appeared. "No, I mean it. I didn't realise how many people would try to use me when I became famous. I don't mean to imply that you would do something like that, but I couldn't help that feeling slinking through me. I know you were only joking."

Viola's eyes softened. "I wasn't thinking. I've not had to deal with people in this realm of life before. I'll try to think before I speak in future."

"You don't have to change yourself for me, Viola.

I need to get out of my own head. I *know* that not everyone is after my money, but it's not always easy to remember. Now, are you ready to try this?"

Viola nodded. She watched as he took a couple of steps back before jumping to the other side. As he landed, he turned to check on her. It wouldn't be as easy for her to copy the same movement. Viola took a few extra steps back than David before she began to run. She pushed off from the edge of the river and launched herself across the gap. Her landing was less graceful. As she teetered back, David reached out and pulled her to safety. Without him, she was sure she would have ended up with more than wet shoes.

Viola attempted to stifle the gasp as their closeness caused her magic to spark through her. From the raised eyebrow, her attempt had failed. His mouth moved as though he wanted to say something, but the words never came as he pulled himself from her.

"Thanks for making sure I didn't end up as a drowned rat." Viola laughed nervously.

"No problem," he said. "To be honest, I'm not sure Tom would be too happy with me if I took you back to the car covered in river water."

Viola smiled wryly. "No, I can't imagine he'd be enthusiastic about the smell, or having to clean it up. At least it would have been river water and not a stagnant puddle."

∗∗∗∗∗∗∗∗∗∗∗∗∗

It didn't take long for the shade of the trees to reach out and cover them. Soon, they were lost within the criss-cross of trunks, hiding them from the outside world. Viola stared in wonder that she'd never made her way to this part before. How long had she been coming here, and she'd managed to miss this piece of hidden safety? As her thoughts consumed her, she felt a slight hum from her hand. She looked down to see David's reaching out to hers. She paused. Before she could overthink it, she took his hand and laced her fingers through his. Her energy seemed to thrum happily against the contact. She hoped it wasn't something he could feel as well. She saw the smile draw across his face before he turned away.

"Is this a proper den we're looking for?" Viola asked.

"Of course," he said. "Are you expecting something half-arsed? It's not a few twigs leaning against each other. We spent a good couple of days getting it right." He looked up and down the row of trees. "I think it's this way."

"You don't remember?"

"I was fourteen. It was half my life ago. I'm allowed to forget some things."

"Seems off if it was your favourite place in the world," she said nonchalantly.

"That's why I remember the trees but not which way through them." He laughed. "Although, I think it was right. I always got it wrong back then as well."

"Lead the way, oh intrepid explorer."

Quicker than she thought, David picked up his pace and pulled her along behind him.

"Now I know I'm in the right part." He let go of Viola's hand and walked towards one of the trees. "See those markings?" he asked, pointing above her head.

Viola squinted. "I don't think I have the same

eyesight as you." She followed the direction of his arm. "Or maybe it's a height thing."

He shook his head. "It's not my eyesight. Here." He tried to point a little above his head. "This is where we notched the tree so we wouldn't forget which way to go." His fingers ran over the marked trunk. "I'd forgotten we'd done that."

Viola watched his face, the shifting emotions as memories ran through his mind. "A smart move from past you, or at least your past friends," she said quietly, not wanting to ruin the moment. "We're almost there?"

"Yeah, we can't be too far now."

He walked a few steps ahead of her, looking around. "Well, I think I've found it. But I'm not sure it's weathered as well as me."

Viola approach ed and laughed when she saw what was left. There were still a few pieces of wood propped through the branches. They looked like they could have been a roof, but there weren't any walls standing.

"I would like to say you've both aged as bad as the other, but even I can't make that comment with a straight face," she said. "You definitely look a lot better than this. A quick fix up and the den will be as good as new. Could be a side project for whenever you're back this way." She turned to look at him.

David smiled at her. "True. Maybe I'd be able to get help on it."

"I don't know. Are you still in touch with your old friends? They might want to pitch in and help restore it," she said, her hand resting lightly on her hip as she through about it.

"I was hoping it would be someone else who would help."

"Oh yeah?"

"Yeah, someone about this tall with dark hair and the most emotive steel blue eyes. Know anyone like that who might want to spend some time in these trees?"

"I think they could be persuaded."

"You sure?" he asked, closing the distance between them.

"They might need to check their diary for when they're free. You should ask them." She gazed up at him.

"Viola." She suppressed the shudder that ran through her body as he said her name. "Would you be willing to spend time with me in these trees, ruining clothes, to put this den back together?"

"Hmm, I'll have to check my diary and get back to you," she said, taking a step back and putting some distance between them.

Her head felt dizzy, and her magic was behaving in a way she'd never experienced before. Her thoughts were torn, scattered. One half wanted to run, to escape from the way she felt. The other wanted to stay, to see what would happen if she let them get closer. It would be easy to fall into this feeling.

"Oh, so you don't want to help." David's voice broke through her internal battle.

"I never said that." She ran her hand against the closest tree, her eyes sparkling at the potential in front of them. "It will be nice to get my hands dirty doing something fun. I'd swap mud for blood or vomit any day of the week." She grimaced.

"You're a doctor?"

"Close, but no cigar. I was tempted to be a doctor,

but I felt more drawn to nursing. It's not half as glamourous as it may sound, but helping people is all I've ever wanted to do."

"You're a bit of a pure soul, aren't you?"

Viola's laugh echoed around them. "I don't think most people would describe me that way. Annoying maybe, reckless as well. But not a pure soul. I want to help those I can."

"If it's worth anything, I'd call you that a lot more than annoying."

"It's better than some of the things I've been called."

David's arm reached out towards her before he dropped it back to his side. "Will you help me restore this den back to its former glory, oh pure soul?"

"Of course! Who would pass up the chance to tell this story to their grandkids?"

Chapter Eight

Viola walked through the door, a smile still on her face. The afternoon had been perfect, and for a moment, all her worries for the coven had melted. She'd felt free and relaxed from helping anyone. Was this how everyone else always felt?

"Mum, are you in?" she called into the darkened house. "Sorry I'm late home. I was on a date. Or at least, I think it was a date."

A noise sounded from the living room.

"Mum?"

Viola tiptoed into the dark room, her energy ready and waiting across her arms. She used a small amount to flick the switch and flood the room in light. Her mum sat motionless in the middle of the room, surrounded by boxes.

"Mum, are you all right?"

Emilia's eyes slowly fluttered open. She looked around her, a small 'o' forming on her mouth.

"Mum?"

"Viola?" She shook her head slowly. "Sorry. I didn't realise how much that would take out of me." A weak smile formed across her face.

Viola squashed the urge to check on her. There was a look on her mum's face that made her look like she didn't want or *need* her help. "What would take it out of you?"

Emilia gestured to the boxes around her. "These are what's left." She took a deep breath. "After your dad did what he did, I hid them. I didn't want anyone else to feel how I did. I didn't want anyone else to grow up without a parent they loved."

Viola's vision blurred. His death had lingered over their family for so long it was easy to forget how much pain could suddenly hit you.

"It's not only notebooks. I packed up everything I could see that was his. I didn't want to deal with it. And I've not been dealing with it."

"You don't have to feel bad," Viola said as she made her way across the room. She took care not to knock and displace anything her mum had retrieved.

"I didn't want you to follow in his footsteps. I wanted you to have the life he wanted for you, but you're stubborn. Just like Alex." Emilia smiled ruefully. "He would have wanted you to have these. They don't make a lot of sense, but you're more determined than I've ever been."

"Thanks, Mum." The words seemed empty and cold from what she had been given. Her mum had always made been proud, but for Viola this showed how much Emilia believed in her. Her eyes began to water but she managed to stop them spilling over.

"No problem, sweetheart. I don't know if they will be useful, but they might help narrow down your options. You're stronger than me, so the ones that aren't wrapped in riddles might be easier for you try. No, don't you contradict me," Emilia said before she could be interrupted. "I've watched you grow into a wonderful young woman, and I've watched your magic grow. You were never happy unless you could push yourself. I can see your dad's determination in you. Maybe that's the type of determination we need to keep surviving."

Viola flung herself at her mum, allowing the tears to pour freely.

"Careful of the books." Emilia laughed, her own tears caressing her cheeks.

"Thanks, for everything. I hope I can make you proud. I hope I would have made him proud."

"Oh, Vi, I'm already so proud of you. The way you choose your own path. The way you always choose the path to help as many as you can. What more could a mum ask for? He would have been proud of you as well. I know you were only five when it happened, but he was already in love with the person you were becoming. Even then, you were keeping us on our toes. Rescuing animals and trying to make everyone feel better. He would have loved to have taught you everything he knew. These books might be able to do what he couldn't."

Viola gingerly pulled one of the books from the nearest box. Her fingers shook slightly as she finally held onto something her dad held dear. Maybe these would be the key to understanding why the protection was failing and how Sophie could have been taken so easily.

"Thank you."

"They were always yours. I should have given them to you sooner." Emilia cleared her throat. "So, you were on a date?"

Chapter Nine

Viola looked at the boxes she'd piled into her room—if you could call it a bedroom anymore. It more closely resembled an abandoned storage locker. How had her dad had time to do anything if he'd filled enough notebooks to half the space within her room? She contemplated the boxes in front of her; she didn't want to admit it, but even one would have been too many for her to look through on her own. She pulled a few from the open box next to her. She flipped through the pages, not taking in any of the information before setting them on her bed. The writing wasn't small at least, but it still didn't mean she would have time to do it by herself.

Her mind wandered back to William's offer. Did he mean it? Would he still be willing to help her? Her feet itched to grab his number from the drawer, but she didn't want to cave. She could do this on her own. She was being silly.

Ebb climbed onto the desk beside her and nudged one of the notebooks.

"You think I should start with this one?" she asked the tabby.

She reached across and picked up the book. There wasn't anything different about this one from the one in her hand. At least, there was nothing that stood out to her. She grabbed a blank piece of paper and started to write out the notes her dad had made. If she put them in her own handwriting, it might make more sense.

Drained, Viola flicked on the landing light as she made her way into the kitchen. The last few hours she had read through as many pages as she could, including the riddles and doodles littered around the more understandable notes. Some of the work he was doing looked fascinating, but her brain refused to make sense of anything. She finally stopped to rest her eyes when Ebb had nudged her. She was hoping all the cat wanted was food, but a witch's familiar didn't usually push her out of her own room for food.

As she made her way around the darkened house, she felt nervous. How long would William wait for her to change her mind? She could do it now; there were more than enough books for them both to go through. Taking that chance now could save weeks of frustration.

"What should I do, Ebb?" she whispered.

"Meow," was the only response she received. She didn't know what else she expected.

She turned the kitchen light on and dished out some food for Ebb. Even if the cat hadn't made her come down here for this reason, it was only fair to give her some reward. When the bowl was placed on the floor, she opened the drawer she'd thrown William's number into. After some searching, she was able to find the scrap of paper. Her fingers trembled as she held it.

Viola grabbed her phone from her pocket and started to write a text.

****

"Thanks for agreeing to meet with me after the other day," Viola said, nursing the warm cup of tea.

"Don't worry about it. I have a tendency to come on a little too strong. But I'm glad you've changed your mind."

"About that." Viola rubbed the back of her neck. "I know I said I could do it on my own, but I think this might take more than one person. If only to read through all the notes."

William drank his coffee. The longer he remained quiet, the more Viola regretted this decision.

"What was it that made you change your mind?"

"What do you mean?"

"You said you thought you could do it alone, but something must have changed. What was it?" His eyes glinted, mischief shining across his face.

Viola picked at the sleeve of her coat. She didn't want to meet his eye. Didn't want to know what reaction he would have to what she needed to tell him. "I might have got hold of my dad's books."

"Really?" The shock in his voice forced her to look at him. William fell back into his chair. "You managed to get them." The way he sat in his chair made her realise that wasn't what he was expecting her to say. He might have wanted her to admit that even she needed help from time to time.

"It wasn't easy," she admitted. "Or, I should say my mum was reluctant to give them to me. But I think she needed a little pushing."

"Stubbornness an Everett trait?"

Viola had the decency to look away. "Look, if you don't want to help, fine. That's on me. But I thought you'd want to know I've changed my mind." Her hand squeezed the warm cup. "I can't do this on my own." The last words came out small, almost pleading.

William laughed. "You're so serious when you're admitting you need help. Is this what you're like with all your friends?"

"We're not—"

William held up his hands. "Don't say something you might regret. What do you need me to do?"

Viola pushed herself further across the table, her body almost leaving the chair she sat on. "My dad wrote the majority of his notes in riddles, and I think doodles." She looked around the café before continuing. "There are a fair few boxes that my mum has passed to me. I'm not sure if it's all writings, but it's enough to need some help. If we can share the notebooks and try to see any patterns, we might be able to figure out what my dad had gotten himself into."

"Doodles and riddles?"

"Yeah. I'm guessing he didn't want anyone else to be able to understand the intricacies of the magic he was conjuring up."

"I guess that would put a slight spanner in the works." William paused. "Do you have information or a copy of a notebook to look through?"

Viola pulled her bag from the floor onto the table. She searched through until she pulled out the one she had been running through herself, along with the notes she'd been making.

"This is what I've got so far. It's not a lot. I've been moving the notes across into my own handwriting to see if there's any repeating patterns or word choices. I've never studied code breaking."

William pulled the notebook across the table and slowly thumbed through the pages, his eyes peering at the notes. "I think I might have an idea with this, but it will take a few days to work through. Is it okay if I take this?"

Viola hesitated but pushed through the worry of losing one of her dad's possessions. "Sure. Do you want these as well?" she asked, fanning out the pages she'd written on.

"Any extra thoughts and ideas will be great to work through."

"Apart from work, I don't have a lot going on, so feel free to drop me a text if you find anything. I'll carry on with another of the books and see if I can find anything in there."

"I think we might have the beginnings of a beautiful plan, Viola," William said, smiling at her.

****

Viola lay on her bed, scooting closer to the circle of light emanating from her bedside lamp. This notebook seemed like nonsense to her as well. No matter how many times she drew out the pictures or wrote the words, she couldn't make any sense of it. She had tried to see if any of the riddles were online, but nothing. Unless she could find a book with the code explained, she didn't have much hope either of them would figure out what her dad had been up to.

Her own notebook was now dotted with doodles as she tried to trick her mind into making sense of what she wrote. No matter how many stars, hearts, or music notes she added around the page, none of them were clearing it up for her.

"C'mon, Dad. You must have done something so someone could read it," she muttered to herself as she flopped onto her back. "Why would you make all these notes so no one else could understand them?"

She let the magic hum across her body and feel across the notebook. She'd already tried this and found nothing. No matter how many times she was met with a void, she couldn't stop herself. If her magic could pick up something on the book, it might help her figure out the code he was using. Maybe there was a piece of him left behind she could use to understand the weird patterns and symbols. They were too deliberate to be anything other than an addition to the riddles he'd done. As much as they looked like doodles on first glance, there was something off about them. They were too precise, not nearly smudged as much as something you'd do absentmindedly. With a groan, she let her magic retreat. Still nothing was showing itself.

As she resolved to stare at the page of squiggles for another hour, she was distracted by the buzzing of her phone.

How do you feel about dinner? D x

Depends on the dinner x

Tomorrow, I'll cook. D x

I can't. Work. Next week? X

Sure. Let me know which day works best for you

and I'll have you picked up and brought by. D x

Perfect x

"You need to be careful here, Vi," she said to herself. There was an easiness to David she'd never experienced before. One she could feel pulling her further under. The more time she spent talking to him, the more she could feel her defences failing. She was letting him in. As much as she tried to remind herself that nothing serious could come from it, it didn't make her want to stop. She wanted to feel free.

Guilt crept through her. David made her forget all about the coven and the worries they were facing. This wasn't the time to be distracted. Especially now she had to decipher a code nobody alive knew. She chewed on her bottom lip. Would it matter if she wasn't fully focused for a day or two? Most of the coven didn't use their magic like her. A few hours of rest wouldn't bring any harm to them. It could even help if her mind was able to relax sometimes. But none of her reasons stopped the guilt.

Chapter Ten

"What time are you leaving tonight?" Emilia asked.

"He said he'd get someone to fetch me at about six p.m.," Viola said, her eyes concentrating on the books in front of her. They lined the edge of the table, with only a small space left for her own notes to sit.

"Do you know where you're going?"

The pen paused above the paper. "No. He said he was going to cook for me, so I'm guessing wherever he's staying." She went back to her notes.

"Vi, let me know as soon as you do."

"Don't worry, Mum. I'll be fine."

She continued flicking between the notebooks, ignoring the stare she could feel from her mum.

"You don't know this man. What makes you think you'll be fine?"

"Trust me. I have a good feeling about this," Viola

mumbled.

Emilia sighed. "I trust you, but I worry about you as well. I don't want to see you getting hurt."

"I'll make sure I'm fine. You know how powerful I am."

"Do not joke about using your magic like that. I know you're powerful, but we don't want you drawing attention to yourself. Or doing something that you can't reverse."

Viola stopped what she was doing. "I would never do anything that would bring too much attention to me. The majority of the coven and I might not have been on the best terms, but I don't want to see anyone get hurt. Anyway, I reckon I could keep myself safe without using my magic."

"That might be true, but don't let yourself get into that situation." Emilia moved around the kitchen, picking up her things. "I'll be out tonight, but if you send me a message, I'll be right there."

Viola laughed. "Go. Have fun. I'll be fine, Mum. I mean, what could a businessman do to a witch?"

✶✶✶✶✶✶✶✶✶✶✶✶✶

Viola pulled at the sleeves of her cardigan. Should she change? If she ran upstairs, she might be able to find something else to wear. She ran through the list of options, unable to decide on anything better.

"Stop being ridiculous. It's only dinner," she said to herself.

She couldn't help it. Her stomach was doing flips and her head felt dizzy. If she didn't know any better, she would have thought she was experiencing her first teenage crush all over again. She fiddled with the edges of her fringe that fell in front of her eyes, pushing them into what she thought was a good style. She glanced at the clock. She was sure her ride should have been here by now.

A knock on the door startled her.

Viola grabbed her bag from the kitchen chair. A smile plastered on her face, one she hoped didn't look as nervous and awkward as she felt. Her thoughts skidded to a stop at the sight of David behind her door. He turned slightly, his fingers ruffling the front of his hair. The other hand held a bouquet of flowers.

He turned to look at her as the door opened. "Hey. I brought you these."

She stared.

"I'm sorry if you don't like them. I wanted to get you something and I saw these and thought of you."

"No, they're perfect." The burning heat of colour slowly rose through her cheeks. She took the bunch from his hands. "Let me put them in some water and I'll be back out."

David nodded at her as she turned and made her way back inside. It took a little longer than she thought. She turned to leave and jumped at David standing behind her. She hadn't heard him follow her in. He didn't notice her looking at him straight away. His attention was taken by something on the table.

"You frightened me," Viola said, her hand over her chest.

"Sorry. I wanted to check you hadn't fainted on me in here."

"No, only a vase emergency."

"Ready?"

Viola nodded. As she passed the table, she realised she had left her notebooks open.

****

"When you said you were making food, I didn't expect this." Viola gestured around the mess on the kitchen sides.

David smiled at her, his grin encapsulating his face. Infectious, she felt her own follow.

"I wanted to woo and impress."

"I think you've got the impress part down," Viola said, sipping at the glass of rosé wine. "Where did you learn to make fresh pasta?"

"At home. I like seeing where I can push myself," David said as he cut the pasta dough into strips. "It's one of the things that's helped me with my businesses." He stopped talking and looked at her. "Sorry. You don't want to hear about all that."

"No, it's interesting finding out about the real David Richardson. The one who isn't performing for TV audiences. How many people can say they've watched you make pasta and then eaten it afterwards?"

David tapped his find on his chin. "I think I've lost count."

Viola almost missed the smile he tried to hide behind his hand. "Very funny," she said, throwing a piece of dough at him.

"Hey, don't waste all the food." He laughed, picking the uncooked pasta from his face.

"I promise that will be my only throw."

"Good."

The silence settled over them, comfortable and

familiar. She didn't realise she could feel so relaxed with someone she barely knew. Her body unfurled into the bar stool; it had been too long since she'd let herself feel like this. She wished she could allow herself this type of comfort and ease more often, but with the potential threat facing the coven, she didn't know if she could let herself.

"Do you need any help with anything? I feel a bit useless sitting here with a glass of wine."

"No, I'm fine. I said I would cook. I'm not going to let my guest do anything when I'm more than capable." He moved the strips into the boiling pot of water on the hob. "Apart from the pasta, the rest of the meal is simple."

Silence wrapped around them again. Viola finished her drink, placing the glass on the side. She didn't want to get too carried away, but she couldn't help the awkwardness she felt. Her thoughts were disrupted by a phone ringing. David raised his eyebrow at whoever had appeared on the front of his phone.

"I'm sorry. Do you mind if I get this?"

"No, go on. Need me to keep an eye on the food?"

David nodded as he answered the phone. "Hi, Father." His carefree tone and playfulness dropped as he walked from the kitchen.

She stirred the pasta and kept an eye on the sauce David had made. It didn't take him long to come back.

"All good?" she asked him.

The corners of his eyes tightened, but he nodded at her. "My father is…" he paused, rubbing the back of his neck. "A difficult man. He never fails to remind me that I'm a disappointment to him and the family. He's always preferred my sister, Georgina, over me. I think he believes she's more amenable to his manipulation. I used to think he was wrong, but I don't know any more."

"I'm sorry," Viola said, her hand laid gently on his arm. "Not all families are what we want to them to be. For what's it's worth, I think you would be someone I'd be proud of."

David smiled weakly at her. "Thanks."

"Any time."

****

"That was the best thing I think I've ever eaten," Viola said as she placed the empty plate on the sideboard.

"You're welcome. I'm glad I remembered all the steps to it."

"I think forgetting a few steps would still be better than anything I've been able to make."

David placed both dishes in the sink. "You said you were a nurse, right? That should be worth more than any home-cooked meal."

"Yeah, but I'm only recently qualified."

"Recently qualified?" His eyebrows furrowed. "The confusing notebook wasn't any studies, then."

"Confusing notebook?" Viola drifted off. "Oh, that? No, not related to anything study wise." She scrambled to think of something to explain it. Anything that wasn't the truth. "I've always had a love of riddles and pictograms, but I think the ones I've looked up recently might be too advanced for me."

"Need any help with them?"

"No. That would be cheating. I've got to figure it out on my own, otherwise it loses the fun."

"If you change your mind, I'm a dab hand at riddles."

"Is there anything you can't do?"

"Hmm, I could probably think of something."

David moved around to her side of the kitchen. He placed his hand over hers as her cheeks reddened at their closeness. Dizziness fell over her as her energy surged to where their bodies touched. She fought to ignore the feeling.

"Thank you for the food," she said, her voice wavering. Her concentration slipped.

"You're welcome, again," he said, his thumb rubbing small circles on the back of her hand.

"I should go home. I have an early start tomorrow." Her voice was barely louder than a whisper in the quiet of the room.

"You can stay if you want," he said in a low voice.

She felt a pull towards him; her body mimicked his. It would only take a small movement to leave no space between them. Would it be so bad if she didn't go home? Would the world end? No, but it would pull her even further from what she needed to concentrate on.

She slowly pulled the humming of her energy away from their contact, but she didn't move her hand. She liked the warmth of him on her. She stood from her seat and placed a small kiss on his cheek.

"As much fun as I feel like it would be to stay, I should go. If you don't mind?"

David shook his head. "I don't mind at all. But I would like to see you again."

Viola smiled. "Next time, I'll cook."

Chapter Eleven

Viola waited in the early evening dusk. She'd been visiting the Peak District more in the past couple of months than she had for the last few years. It didn't take William long to join her, despite the strange directions she had given him.

"Hi, Will. Hope it wasn't too much of a pain to find."

"I may have taken a wrong turn, but that's on my map reading skills. I hope you don't mind, but I've brought someone with me. Part of my plan I was working on," he said.

She looked behind him and saw Casey trailing in his steps. Her annoyance flared, but she tried to keep it from her face. "No, it's not a problem. We need as many people as possible if we want this to work. Hi, Casey," she added stiffly.

"Hey." The other woman looked past her. "Will didn't mention it was you he was meeting."

The almost biting chill from the late spring breeze bit more as Viola and Casey looked at each other. Viola fought the urge to say something she would regret.

"We need to get out of the hills as much as possible, but it's easy enough to find somewhere private."

"Good call."

"I guess you have somewhere in particular to go if you were going to drag us all the way out here."

"Not too far. We need somewhere that isn't overrun. Although where isn't at six p.m. on a Wednesday?"

Viola set off, hoping the other two would follow. She was a little annoyed she hadn't been given a heads up about Casey. They had never been in agreement in their lives. But she couldn't blame William. He hadn't grown up with the two of them. He might not have realised how divided they were.

"How did you find this place?" William asked, the words breaking through her thoughts.

"The Peak District?" Viola laughed.

"Yeah, the Peak District." She could almost hear his eyes rolling. "No, this specific place."

"I come out here to think and practice. It's nicer to connect with the energy when you're out in the open. Pushing its limits without worrying about who might see you, or what could cause an issue. It's freeing. I've always found that being outside helps me with any new magic I'm working through. Plus, it makes me feel like one of the witches you read about. The ones in sync with nature."

"The ones dancing naked around fires?"

"Of course that would be the bit you would take

from that."

"The pictures stick in your mind a lot more than the words do."

"William, what is wrong with you?" Casey said, speaking for the first time since they set off.

"Nothing. But you can't show those pictures to young teens and expect them not to be mesmerised."

"Luckily, we're here, so you can stop fantasising about naked women dancing in the woods." She looked pointedly at William. "And no, we won't be doing that now either."

"Probably a good shout."

"What's the plan?" Casey asked as Viola stopped them to set out her blanket.

"I've seen something I think we should try. If we want to be able to work together, we need to recognise each other. Or at least at each other's individual signatures. It will make anything else we do easier when we need all of our efforts to be combined." She sat on one side of the blanket and gestured for the others to sit as well.

"Are you not going to say what it is?"

"This is the thing. I'm not one hundred percent sure what it is. But the starting point should definitely be more understanding of each other."

Casey rolled her eyes. "You brought us all the way out here to open ourselves up to each other. Did we need to be here for this?"

"Safety is the main thing. Here, we're not near any of the coven members or many people. It's also my go-to place to practise magic away from prying eyes."

"What have you been up to?" William asked. He shuffled closer to her. "You can tell us. We won't tell anyone."

"Speak for yourself," Casey scoffed.

Viola ignored the mumbled snark. "I've got a few things I've been theorising about, but I've not had the chance to expand it anything more than an idea. I've not mentioned these plans to my mum. I'm worried about what she might say." She sighed and leaned back on her arms. "But we might as well try to focus."

"So, relax and feel for the magic?" William asked.

"I guess."

Casey raised an eyebrow at them. "Just relax?"

"I know my magic works better if I've had time to channel into it. It might not work for everyone, but it's a good place to start. I'm going to let mine rise to the surface and you two see if you can sense it. Everyone's magic feels different, so you should be able to feel it."

"And after that?" Casey probed.

"I've not got to that part in the notes. I don't know if this will work yet." She took a deep breath to steady herself. "Are you ready?"

"Of course," William said.

"Okay."

Viola centred herself on the ground. She used the stillness of the trees around her as a calming anchor. She didn't want to fall too far into meditation, but it needed to be enough. A few deep breaths later and she could feel her energy moving from the well within her. Its warmth flooded her body. If she pressed gently, she could feel the energy in the world around her.

"Try now," she murmured.

She tried not to tense as she felt their strange signatures bumping into her energy. There was a closeness to it she wasn't expecting. She shuddered. It felt as though she was being exposed to the other two. She didn't realise allowing another to find her magic would cause such an effect.

"Did anyone else feel that?" William asked.

"The weirdly intimate touch of someone else's energy?" Viola asked. She saw both nod. "I guess we know why people don't do this."

"What can we do with this? What's the purpose of understanding each other?" Casey asked.

"It's one way to make sure that we know who is doing what. If we need to create anything long lasting, if we know how the other's energy feels, we will be able to tell if it's safe."

"Did anyone find their magic wanted to link? You know linking isn't allowed within the coven. Abigail would never agree to that," Casey asked, a frown forming on her face. She rubbed the goosebumps from her arms.

"Ms. Glorian might not get to make that choice," Viola said.

"Easy there. No one said we would need to link our energies together," William said.

"He's right. I don't think that's what my dad did. If he had, it would mean there were other people in the coven who would have an idea of the magic he was attempting, and no one has been vocal about that." She paused. "Although, it will have to be something we stay aware of. We don't want to accidentally create a link. It doesn't feel like it's something just anyone should do."

"I agree. Who knows what that could end up doing. Maybe something has been written about this before. I think we should check whatever documents we can get hold of before we carry on," Casey agreed as she stood up, dusting the dirt from her jeans.

"Is that everything?" William asked.

"Yeah, that was as far as I got. I know it's not a lot, but it's also good magic practice." Viola stood. "Did you have any luck with the notebook?"

He shook his head. "Nothing made sense to me."

"What notebook?" Casey asked.

"I managed to get a hold of my dad's old notebooks, but he wrote non-standard spells in riddles, or codes, or some secret language. It's not making any sense, and I asked William to help look through them with me."

"Have you got any on you now?"

Viola shook her head. "I didn't think I would need to bring any out with me."

Casey sighed. "Would you be okay with me getting a ride back with you? I can pick up a couple and make a start on them."

Viola stared. "What?"

"If I'm going to help, I'm going to need to be able to see what Alex was doing as well. I didn't come all the way out here for the fun of it."

Viola didn't know how to reject her offer without being as rude as she wanted. "Yeah, sure," she said through gritted teeth. "Three pairs of eyes would be better than two."

William beamed at them both. "I knew you two would get along if you gave each other a chance."

Viola barely stopped her eyes from rolling. "Yeah, we'll be great friends."

Casey snickered.

"Before you go, have you tried talking to any of the other coven members?" William asked.

"No, why?"

"Someone older than us had to know what your dad was doing. Is it likely that he would have gone rogue and not told anyone?"

"I mean, looking at his notes, I'd say it could be likely. Why would you be so cryptic if you were sharing all your plans with everyone?"

William dropped his head. "I guess you're right. Still, it's worth asking around."

"I'll see what my mum has to say. Do you want to ask anyone you think might answer?"

"I'll let you know how it goes."

"I'll check with my family as well," Casey added. "They've never spoken about your family, but they might know something."

✱✱✱✱✱✱✱✱✱✱✱✱✱

"When you said you'd been given a lot of books, I didn't think you meant this many."

Viola groaned. "I know. I don't know how he had the time to practise with how many notes he took." She pulled one of the boxes closer to her. "Don't get me wrong, I'm glad I have so many things that were his, but I don't think there's enough time in life to read through and understand everything he wrote. It's not helping us to find what he did to protect us." She rummaged through the box, moving aside anything that looked less like a notebook. "Here, take these." She held out her hand, the notebooks pointed towards Casey. She tried to ignore the way they shook slightly.

Casey moved to them, but Viola jerked her arm back. "Wait. Before you take them, can I ask one thing?"

"What?"

"Can you not write in these? I want to keep them as close to how he left them as possible."

Casey gently plucked the paper from her grasp. Viola stared at where Casey's hand had brushed against her fingers. A familiar surge of energy ghosted over her hand. She looked at her as she started talking.

"I promise I won't write in them." She tucked them into her canvas bag. "I don't know what you think of me, but I wouldn't ruin something that was so important to anyone. I feel honoured that you're trusting me with them as it is. I thought you would refuse."

Viola shifted on her leg. "I almost did. But I don't think I can go through all of these on my own, even if William is helping me." She exhaled deeply. "If you manage to make any sense of what he wrote, let me know."

"Of course. I'll get your number from Will."

"One second." Viola manoeuvred to her desk and scrawled her number on one of the discarded scraps of paper. "This way, you've got it without needing to wait."

Casey took the scrap. "He'd have given it up, but now you know I have it. If I see anything that makes sense, I will make sure to contact you as soon as I can."

"Thank you," Viola forced herself to say. "I know we've not been friendly before, but I'm glad William has asked you to help. I know you're good at what you do."

A strange emotion flickered over Casey's face, and Viola couldn't pick up a read on the other woman's emotion. "Making sure the coven stays safe is one of the most important things. But thanks for thinking I will be of help."

Chapter Twelve

er head ached from the late nights, but Viola knew it would be worth it. Even without understanding the majority of what was written, she saw a glimpse into her dad's mind. Was he always so enigmatic? From the pieces of her memories, she only remembered the cuddles and smiles. She wished she could have known him. If he had lived longer, she might have had less headaches.

She pushed all thoughts of her dad and his notebooks from her mind as she entered the hospital. The usual bright feeling that emanated from the halls and rooms was lost. There was something wrapped around the place. It wasn't something she could put her finger on, but a chill settled on her. Worry wormed its way into her mind. The slithering feeling of anxiety pulled at her. Her energy responded to the fear. Primordial, anticipating the next move, she fought to keep it from spilling out. Something was wrong.

Something was very, very wrong.

"It's okay, relax," she told herself. "There's nothing to worry about. It's a normal day at work. There isn't anything causing your energy to work against you." She took a few deep breaths in the hopes they would calm the fear that was slowly building inside her.

She took the quickest route to the staff room. After throwing her belongings in her usual cupboard, she headed on her rounds. A few small steps from the room had Viola wanting to run out of the building. Her fear shifted to dread. Her energy hummed beneath her skin, its tell-tale glow appearing in patches.

The further she moved into the corridor, the more the feeling crashed over her, threatening to pull her under. Her skin itched. She felt exposed. Fear flashed through her again. She steadied her legs, willing her emotions back. Viola knew she was stronger than this. She wouldn't let herself fall into them. Not here, not where she could endanger anyone. The only way to get through this would be to stay calm.

"Easy enough to think," she mumbled.

Her body didn't want to behave. If anything, it wanted to rebel and worry about the consequences later. It didn't matter how far down the corridor she got, the feeling of being watched and exposed followed her. She turned at the end of the corridor and bumped into Rachel.

"Oof, sorry. I didn't see you there, Vi." Rachel took a step back and looked at her friend. "Are you okay?"

"Yeah, I'm fine." Viola waved her off.

"You sure? You look like something's on your mind."

With a smile she didn't feel, she said, "Yeah, I'm

good. I've been thinking about my dad. You know how it is."

A soft smile appeared on Rachel's face. "No wonder we both missed each other. Need any help with your rounds today?"

"No, I should be fine, thanks. I'll catch you later."

As Rachel turned to leave, Viola stopped her. "Wait. Does the hospital feel weird to you today?"

"Weird?"

"Yeah. I got a strange feeling when I walked in."

"No, I've not noticed anything."

Viola turned and headed towards her usual rounds. The feeling didn't completely leave her, but after her encounter with Rachel, she felt safer. If the feeling was coming from a person in the hospital, maybe they had decided to leave her alone. She could only hope they would stay away.

The frenzy of her energy ebbed as her shift passed by. She had gone about her rounds without any issues. Every so often, she would feel a slight brush of whatever, or whoever, was watching her, but it was subtle. A ghosting feeling of a spider web catching on her arm.

"Still feeling strange?" Rachel joked as she retrieved her things for the day.

"No. It must have been the thoughts of my dad." The lie slipped through Viola's lips with ease.

"You're looking better. Maybe you needed to get out of your thoughts for a bit."

"Hmm," Viola responded noncommittally. "You in tomorrow?"

"Of course."

"Oh, to have more than a day off between shifts."

"To have more than a few hours."

"I'll see you tomorrow," Viola said as she left the room.

She took another few steps and the feeling hit her again. It wasn't as strong as it had been a few hours ago, but it was enough to make her energy thrum. She looked around the corridor. There wasn't anything out of place. She took a few steps back. The feeling didn't leave, but it didn't feel as strong either. She checked no one else was coming up this way. She didn't want to explain what she was doing.

When she knew she was alone, she let her bag drop to the floor. Viola stood still, her eyes closed. Her energy slowly coaxed along her body. As soon as the energy reached her fingertips, she let it twist out from her. It slowly scanned the nearest wall.

She let her energy move as quickly as she could; she didn't want to spend more time than necessary up here. Just as she was about to give up, she felt it. It was small. She picked up her bag, trying to keep a hold of the location. She held her hand up against the wall and found a slight raised lump. If she hadn't used her magic, she wasn't sure she'd have found it.

****

Viola took a deep breath before knocking on the door. This could either be the best decision for her coven, or the biggest mistake for herself. She hadn't called ahead of her visit and wasn't sure if Ms. Glorian was even at home, but she needed to speak with her.

"Just a minute," the shrill tone called through the door. A couple of seconds passed before the sound of the door being unlocked reached her ears. "Hello, Ms. Everett. How can I help you this evening?"

Viola tried to ignore the cool gaze levelled at her. "I was hoping I could discuss something important with you."

"Come in, come. I will bring a pot of tea through."

Viola was shown into the same sitting room as her initiation had been. It seemed larger without the coven squished inside it. She perched on the edge of the sofa as she waited for her host to return.

"Milk and sugar are in the accompanying jug and dish," Ms. Glorian said as she placed a tea tray on the small table by Viola's side. "Please, help yourself."

"Thank you," Viola said, picking up one of the cups and adding a splash of milk.

"What has brought you to my door today?"

She took a small sip of her drink. "I don't know how to explain it, but I knew you would want to hear this as soon as I could get it to you." She steadied herself. "Something was unsettling at the hospital today, Ms. Glorian. As soon as I entered the place, there was something wrong about it. I couldn't figure it out. At the end of my shift, I had the weirdest sensation fall over me when I left the staff room. I traced it back to a small piece of magic which had been placed on an imperfection on the wall. It had my magic reacting on its own. It wanted to fight back as though there was some danger there. Luckily, I was able to control it," Viola added hastily. "It made me feel vulnerable, weak. I don't know who placed it there, but I will keep an eye on it."

"That seems like quite the story, Viola," Ms. Glorian said as she placed her teacup back on its saucer.

"Was there anything in particular you can remember about this energy?"

"It felt like it was watching me. Like it knew what I am and was waiting for me to reveal myself."

"I see."

"Is there anything we can do about it? Is there anything we can put in place to stop it causing more havoc on everyone?"

"The hospital is no concern of ours," Ms. Glorian chided. "We must protect the coven from whatever this entity is. Thank you for bringing it to my attention. I would suggest you take a few days from work until we can ensure there is no threat to the coven."

"You want me to stop working and leave whatever's in there?" Viola stared at her Elder. "If I don't go back in, won't it look worse? The person, or being, or thing that's in there might realise I've not gone back and decide it was me it was looking for anyway."

Ms. Glorian seemed to ponder over her words. "Of course, we don't want them to find out where you are. Continue as normal, but do not do anything to lessen the magic. It can't know we have found them." She stared at Viola, the force of the look causing her to look away.

"Of course, Ms. Glorian." Viola swallowed down the bile. "Anything to keep the coven safe."

✱✱✱✱✱✱✱✱✱✱✱✱✱

She tried not to slam the door as she stormed into her room, but her conversation with Ms. Glorian had soured her mood. Not do anything to help the hospital? Leave the magic in place? She couldn't sit idly by when she knew there was something more at play. She didn't even know if the magic only affected her, or if it would eventually spread out to everyone. It frustrated her more that she didn't know what she could do to resolve this.

"Viola, what's all the noise for?" her mum called from the hallway.

Viola ignored her, unsure if she would be able to answer without berating their coven Elder. She flopped into bed, pulling the pillow over her face. It didn't take long for her mum to enter the room.

"Vi, love. What's wrong?" Her mum's words caused tears to spring to her eyes. Despite her twenty-five years, she felt like a child again.

"It's not fair, Mum," Viola said as sobs punctuated her breathing. "I'm not supposed to do anything, but I can't leave people to suffer. I don't know what to do."

"Okay, start from the beginning. I feel like there's a lot of information I'm missing."

Viola spilled her heart out to her mum, the anguish twisting through her words. Emilia sat in stunned silence as the tale was recanted.

"She told you to leave the hospital alone?"

"She told me to call in sick and stay away," Viola responded.

Emilia's face had slowly changed from concern to annoyance. "Can you remember what it felt like? The magic you found. Would you be able to tell it apart from someone else's?"

"I think so. It wasn't one I recognised, so it can't be anyone in the coven. It was strong, Mum." Viola screwed up her face. "Much stronger than I've encountered before. It was watching me so far from that spot. I don't know how it did it."

"Did it have any particular signature to it?"

"I don't know what you mean."

"Never mind, darling." Her mum waved her off.

"No, Mum. What is it? What do you think it is?"

Viola could see the hesitation flickering through her eyes. It danced around her face before it disappeared. Her eyes held a hard edge to them, determination settling across her features.

"I don't know for sure, but I know your dad was looking into something strong and powerful. It was why he spent so much time creating that damn protection spell. To keep us safe from something he couldn't understand."

"You knew what Dad was looking into this entire time?" Her disbelief plastered itself on her face. After all the claims her mum had made and she could have helped.

"No. I only knew there was something he was searching for, but he wouldn't tell me what it was. He didn't want me getting caught up in it."

"Did you ever tell any of the coven that he was worried? Why have you never told me this before?"

"I couldn't. I didn't know what it was, and I knew I would never be able to finish his work. I never had a tenth of the strength he possessed, and when he went out, our powers lessened. With the fear that any one of us could be next, we stopped using it. It's why Abigail has never warmed to you. She knows you keep up your practice. She probably fears you as the strongest among us. But it makes me so proud. It would have made your dad proud if he could see the woman you've become. You refuse to bow down, and you're always helping those in need." Emilia took a deep breath and pulled Viola's hand into her own. "Which is why I need you to know I will do whatever it takes to help you with his books, and to keep the hospital safe. I will lend you my energy. Hopefully, we'll be able to break it down together."

"What about Ms. Glorian?"

"I couldn't care less what she thinks. This isn't just about keeping our coven safe. This is about doing what's right and proving we have some humanity left to save. How can we sit by when something could be causing havoc and pain for hundreds?"

"Thank you."

"No, Viola. Thank you for reminding me of what we should be doing."

Chapter Thirteen

The sun was out when Viola woke. It had been a few days, and the sense of dread had been following her through the hospital, but she hadn't done anything to stop it. Her mum might have wanted to help, but she couldn't risk letting the person behind it know she knew. On her first day off in a while, she knew what she wanted to do and where she would go to do it.

After a small hike, Viola reached the den David had shown her. He'd not mentioned it since, but it was remote enough that she didn't worry about anyone seeing her. It had been a couple of weeks, and she had managed to work out some small patterns. Some of the drawings followed certain pieces of writing. It might have been nothing, but she wasn't about to pass up the chance to work it out.

With her usual practice blanket spread out on the ground, she pulled the notebook she had been working in onto her lap. The sun dappled on the pages, obscuring some of her notes. Not that she would move now.

"Okay, so maybe this drawing is how the magic is supposed to feel," Viola said as she closed her eyes.

She concentrated on the magic and thought of the drawing. She pushed the energy from her hands and felt the threads of them hovering in the air. A couple of twists and turns and she felt like the magic was in the places she'd seen. She squinted slightly at the page, her attention split between both tasks. As she looked at the image, her control slipped, and the energy fell into her.

"Focus," she told herself. She shook out the tension from her arms and stretched her body upwards in an attempt to loosen her shoulders.

She pulled the image to the front of her mind. She struggled to keep it there, the shape flitting and sliding around. The idea of it remained, and Viola hoped it would be enough to move her magic to the shape of it. Again, she felt the magic rise through her. The threads waited for her touch. She turned them on themselves. They wove together to form a single thread. She moved it. It slid through the air with more ease than she anticipated. Her control wavered from the shock.

"What was he trying to do with this?" she muttered as she flicked through the pages.

It had taken her too long to realise the simple line drawing in the notebook resembled a piece of wool, and even longer to realise it was how the magic had been twisted on itself. If only the words made more sense. If her dad hadn't written everything in riddles and his own coded language, she might have been able to make some steps forward into strengthening the protection. She shook her head. There was no point in wishing for things that couldn't be changed.

"I wish I could speak to you, Dad," she whispered. "I wish you could give me a sign I'm on the right track. That we'll be able to get through this and keep everyone safe."

She collapsed against the blanket, the notebook clutched to her chest, when an idea hit her. She hadn't checked the notebooks for any traces of her dad's magic. She pushed herself up and placed the notebook in front of her crossed legs. Any trace might be enough for her to have a clue as to what he'd been doing, and where he'd placed the protection.

Tentatively, she let her energy envelop the book. It glided over the object, searching for anything that might have been left over. Nothing.

Frustrated, she fell back onto the blanket. Why couldn't he have done something to it? Anything would have worked. But this wasn't his only notebook. Maybe he'd done something to one of the many others in the boxes.

"I guess I'll have to let William and Casey know what's up," she said aloud.

She should have told them what she had planned, but she didn't want to. Although three people working on something would make it go quicker, she felt crowded. She'd never needed help before, and she'd grudgingly asked for one person's help to be confronted with another. It was too different to how to how she'd spent her life. Despite her reservations, she pulled her phone from her pocket and tapped out a message to both of them. She didn't know whether she should include the way she could pick up on different energy types. It wasn't something a lot of witches learnt, and she didn't want them to think she'd been spying on everyone's magic. How could she explain it? No. She shook her head. She would only tell them if she needed to.

****

Viola was almost packed up when she heard a noise coming towards her. She pulled her magic around herself. If there was anything out there, she knew she'd be able to stop it and would have enough time to leave. Not that she wanted to announce herself to the world, but if it meant the difference between her survival and a potential attack, she would do it without thinking.

She pulled her bag onto her back and pressed herself onto the closest tree. Someone could still sneak up on her, but at least her back was protected. She softened her breathing as the sound moved closer. Branches snapped and leaves rustled as she counted the seconds. She could still hear birds in the treetops above her.

She didn't have to wait much longer as the source of the noise stepped in front of her. Her body sank. "David, I didn't expect to see you here."

David turned to her, eyebrows raised. "I could say the same about you. I didn't know this was your sanctuary from the city."

Viola laughed, the adrenaline trying to leave her body through the noise. "No. Well, not this spot usually. But I do like to come out here. It's quiet and I get away from everything."

David nodded. "I understand. Have you been here long?"

"I was leaving until I heard you coming. You didn't half give me a fright."

He chuckled. "Apologies. If I'd known anyone was here, I'd have had my megaphone to alert them."

"That would be a good idea for next time. You don't know who else you might stumble into around here. It's a perfect spot for a picnic."

"Oh, is that what you were doing?"

Viola laughed again, her nerves finally easing up. "No, only relaxing. But a picnic blanket fits great." She started to move in the direction David had come from. "I hope you enjoy the rest of your afternoon."

"I can't convince you to stay a little longer?" It may not have been a fully conscious effort but he pouted slightly as he asked.

"I wouldn't want to intrude."

"Not at all. Unless you have somewhere to be." His tone was sincere. She couldn't see anything in his face that would make her feel like an unwanted addition to his day.

Viola paused. She wasn't expected anywhere for a while, and she'd not heard back from either Casey or William. "Sure. Do you want me to get out the blanket?"

****

She checked her phone as she walked into the house. Since driving home, she'd only had one new message.

You think we need to make our energies work in sync?

Would that keep the protection locked together? Or do the energies need weaving together? W

She stopped. Could that be what his notebooks were trying to tell her? No one had mentioned her dad working with anyone else. It was always Alex on his own, saving the coven. If Will was right, he wouldn't have needed to do that. Nope, it didn't make any sense. If anyone else knew what he'd done, they wouldn't be keeping quiet now, would they?

"Mum?" she called into the house.

Silence. This was something she knew she should ask about. Was there a way to link everyone's energy? She knew the initiation accepted the energies into the coven, but they weren't bound to each other. Only they would be able to recognise when someone was a friend. Or at least when someone belonged to the same group as them.

I think we need to try and question anyone we can. They might know if my dad was working with anyone else on this protection. Also, I found something out, but maybe we need to meet to talk about it. Vi

Ooh, this sounds exciting. When is everyone free and where should we meet? W

Viola placed her phone on the kitchen table. Ebb rubbed against her leg, asking for food, she presumed. If her mum knew that her dad was worried about something, she might know if there were any people he was working with. Was it her? Had her dad and mum intertwined? She shook the thought from her head. If her mum knew anything about this, she would have mentioned it before.

Her phone buzzed.

Tomorrow, 8pm. Meet at my house. Casey

Chapter Fourteen

Viola knocked on the door. The twilight glow masked her on the front step. It was a little before eight, but she didn't want it to seem like she didn't care. She fidgeted with the edge of her jacket and shifted her weight from her right leg to her left. Should she wait or knock again? The decision was taken from her as Casey opened the door.

"You're early," the other woman said to her.

"Is that all right?"

Casey sighed. "It will have to be. I'm just finishing up some food."

Viola wished there was some form of magic she could do to break the tension between the two of them. Nothing she had tried before had worked, and she didn't want to do anything to mess up Casey's house. She followed her into the small kitchen.

"You can sit," Casey said, gesturing at one of the empty chairs.

Viola took the seat opposite her at the small table. She looked around the room. It gave her a glimpse into the person Casey was. There were pictures of her family on the wall and letters piled up on the counter.

"William shouldn't be too much longer."

Casey didn't respond.

Viola pulled her phone from her pocket, looking over a message David had sent her. A smiled etched across her face. She needed to get over this infatuation. It couldn't lead anywhere, not without revealing what she was. Her energy lurched at the thought.

"Watch it," Casey said, her face pale.

"What?"

"Whatever you're doing with your magic. Cut it out. It's making me feel sick."

"I'm not doing anything," Viola said, the smile falling from her face.

"Well, it's doing something."

Viola paused. She concentrated on keeping her energy in check. "Wait, can you feel when someone uses their magic?"

Casey grimaced. "Clearly. So can you knock it off?"

Her brows furrowed as she pushed her energy down, locking away the easy access she was used to. "What does it feel like? And I'm sorry. I didn't realise anyone could do it, or what it would do to anyone that could."

"It doesn't affect me when I'm expecting it, only when it surges, or I'm caught off guard." Casey stared at her. "I don't normally have to protect myself in my own home. But it's like a buzzing sensation. It rushed around me."

"Sorry, I never knew."

"Why would you?" Casey muttered.

"Can I try something?" Viola asked.

"Like what?"

"Give me your hand." Casey glared at her. "It's not like I'm trying to kiss you or anything."

"In your dreams," Casey said as she raised her arm towards her.

As soon as her palm made contact with her bare flesh, Viola let the energy rush back to the surface and dropped her usual guard. A spark hummed through them. Casey's eyes widened.

"Did you know it would do that?"

"It's only done it with one other person," Viola said, letting her hand drop. "It's almost like an electric shock."

"A little," Casey said, rubbing her fingers over her palm. "What did the other person say about it?"

"They've not mentioned, but they aren't a witch. I know. I don't know what to make of it either," she said before Casey could interject. "I thought it was just a one off, but it happened a couple of times and I've not been able to find any research on it. You've never felt that before?"

Casey shook her head. "I've never noticed, and I think I would notice that. It felt like a surge of energy where you touched me."

"Maybe we can add that to the list of things to research."

Casey made a slight noise but didn't make any other acknowledgements.

Silence dropped over them. The two had never been friends, had never spent much time together, but Viola knew better than to annoy someone in their own home. Especially after shocking them. Viola shifted in her chair. When a knock sounded at the door, she almost jumped from her seat in relief.

"We might as well talk in the living room. There's more space for us in there," Casey said, leading Viola through the house. "Plus, it's warmer."

"What was so urgent we needed to talk about this in person?" William asked as he collapsed into the armchair.

Casey nodded. "Why couldn't it have been a text?"

"My mum told me my dad was looking into something really bad." Viola took a deep breath. "She didn't say what it was, but she was freaked out. She only told me after I let her know about something weird at work. I've never heard of anyone mentioning my dad looking into anything other than the protection. Have you heard anything else?"

"When did she tell you this?"

"A few days ago," Viola admitted.

"A few days and now you tell us," Casey said, glaring at Viola. "Why didn't you tell us straight away? What else do you need to tell us?"

Viola had the grace to look uncomfortable. "I'm not used to having people to talk to about this stuff. I'm getting used to it."

"No excuse. We're supposed to be working together to keep the coven safe, but you're just being you—" Casey said.

"Casey," William interrupted. "She told us, didn't she?"

"No, Will. That's not the point. She needs to know that she can't keep things to herself." Casey turned back to Viola. "You can't run around putting other people in danger and not tell anyone when something important comes up. You can't ignore people. You're not that special or important. You're a self-centred, stuck-up bitch who thinks she can do what she wants. I was willing to give you a chance, but everyone was right. You make everything about you. It's not only you who can keep people safe. There's already one missing person out there, and you don't tell us that something worse could be out there. Unbelievable."

Viola's vision blurred. "Sorry to have bothered you with this." She grabbed her discarded coat and raced from the room.

"Viola, wait," William called behind her, but she was already leaving the house.

She knew they judged her, but she didn't know how deep it ran. The tears fell freely as rushed along the road. The sly looks and barbed words had followed her through the meetings while she grew up, but she thought they were turning a corner. Thought that maybe Casey was starting to see her as the person she was and not the whispered comments she believed. *Stupid*, that was what she'd been. She needed some time away from everyone. She would concentrate as much as possible on what needed to be done, but she couldn't do that right now.

****

Her room was cold. The window had been left open, and Viola didn't have the strength to close it. She'd lay on her bed, wide awake, for too many hours. Sleep was avoiding her, like she was avoiding the incessant buzzing of her phone. As soon as she'd returned home, she'd regretted leaving. She'd proved them right. She'd made the disagreement about her. Her own pride had got in the way of making some headway.

The tears had dried on her face, leaving small tracks down her cheeks. She thought she was over caring what anyone thought of her or what she did, but that wasn't the case. There hadn't been a time she could remember when someone hadn't been talking about her and judging her for what she was doing. She wrapped her arms around her body and squeezed her hands into her ribs. A small sob escaped her as she tried to understand why she hadn't been given the chance to be her own person to anyone else in the coven. Would anyone ever see her as Viola, rather than Alex's daughter? She knew that was the root of why she was judged by everyone.

She moved to close her window before climbing back into bed and pulling the covers back up over her. She didn't want people to negatively judge her for her abilities, and the best way to do that would be to sort things out with Casey and William. Whatever her dad had been up to was too complex for one person on their own to understand. She needed them, as much as she hated to admit it. Even in the dark, on her own, she knew she needed to find a way to make things right. Petty arguments could wait.

Chapter Fifteen

Everyone piled into Ms. Glorian's small living room. Viola had seen William. He'd beckoned to her, but she shook her head at him. They still hadn't spoken since the fight at Casey's, and she didn't know how to deal with the awkwardness. Casey had ignored her completely, even after William had nudged her. She didn't need to spend any time in the frosty silence that would fall over them. What could she say to make things right? She didn't think it should be her to make amends, but it would help to get them all back on speaking terms.

"Hello," Ms. Glorian started. "This will only be a brief meeting today, but feel free to stay afterwards if you need to talk through anything further."

The coven settled down.

"We've not had any more news from High Peak regarding the missing woman, but we are doing what we can to find her. The police were contacted, but so far, they have been unwilling to help as much as we'd hoped. If anyone has any worries or concerns over this, please know we are listening to you and we are doing what we need to."

With no mention of Viola's concerns about the hospital, she drifted off. She wasn't surprised it was overlooked. She was starting to see a pattern with anything that could help, but she couldn't keep focus as Ms. Glorian started talking through some more mundane matters of the coven. The training and improvements being made by the rest of the coven didn't mean a lot if they weren't given the chance to help anyone. This would have been a smaller issue than the larger, more important one of keeping the protection going.

As people started to leave the room, she took her chance.

"Ms. Glorian, can I speak with you for a second?" she asked as she approached the Elder.

"Of course," she responded, although Viola was sure she would rather not. "Is this regarding the hospital?"

"No. I've been looking into what my dad was doing. I want to help in whatever way I can, but I can't find any records or mentions of what he was doing."

"He never told anyone."

"Not even the Collection of Elders?" Viola asked, the disbelief showing to everyone left in the room.

"No," Ms. Glorian said after a slight pause. "He didn't want to worry anyone or have anyone feel like they needed to help."

"Did anyone help him?"

"Not that was mentioned to me."

Viola stood still. She could tell Ms. Glorian was lying, but she couldn't accuse her in front of everyone without proof. "Thank you," she forced herself to say. "Hopefully, I will be able to find the information I need elsewhere." Ms. Glorian inclined her head, but before she could walk off, Viola added, "But if you knew something and didn't help, whatever happens to either coven is partially on you."

Ms. Glorian didn't respond before she moved to another group of witches.

"What was that about?" William asked as he came up behind her shoulder.

"Nothing."

"You doing the solo warrior thing again?"

Viola sighed. "No. I thought that I could get her to help. But I was wrong."

William stared at her.

"I thought of all the people in the coven she may have known what he was researching and would be able to point us in the right direction."

Understanding dawned on his face. "Alex?"

Viola nodded.

"I think she's been trying to save face. A lot of people blamed her, that she didn't put a stop to what he was doing. I've heard people say that if she had, he wouldn't have ended up dead. She's not going to tell his daughter anything that might implicate her any further in the coven's eyes."

"You're right. I thought she might want to do something. Anything to help keep us safe from what's happening now." Viola pushed her fingers through her fringe. "I want someone else to care."

"We do care, Vi," William said, placing his hand on

her shoulder. "We're here for you. What Casey said the other day was in anger."

"It doesn't mean it's not what she or everyone else really thinks."

"And if it is, you can prove them wrong. We need to work together to make it safe for everyone. Maybe you need to stop being so isolated and realise we can help. It might stop the grey hairs."

Viola's hand rushed to her head before she saw the laughter in William's eyes. "Very funny."

"I am. Stop trying to be a lone wolf and you'll find out."

****

Viola settled onto the sofa with Ebb curled up by her feet. The TV was on, but it might as well have been white noise for all the attention she was paying to it. Her conversation with Ms. Glorian replayed through her head. The disinterest from the coven leader was something she couldn't get past. It had been her who had encouraged the rest of the coven to practise, but she didn't want to do the one thing that could help them more than anything. What little respect was left for her dwindled by the second.

"Want to talk about it?" Emilia asked her, handing her a cup of hot chocolate.

"No," Viola mumbled, taking a sip of the hot goodness in front of her.

"It's better to share the issue rather than bottling it up and letting it eat away at you."

"Why does everyone keep saying that to me?"

"Because you don't let anyone in," her mum said,

smiling sadly.

"I don't trust Ms. Glorian. I don't think she wants the protection working again, or at least she's willing to let it disappear if she doesn't have to admit any wrongdoing with Dad. I know she knows something."

"Why do you think she knows anything about what Alex was doing?"

"After asking her, I'm convinced there's something she's refusing to say. If she knows what we can do to keep everyone safe but refuses…" Viola stopped herself before she said something she might regret.

"She didn't want him to do it," Emilia whispered.

Viola stared at her mum. "What?"

"He told her something of what he intended to do. But she didn't want him to. She told him he was a fool, would get himself killed. I guess she was right."

"Did he ever tell you what he told her?"

Emilia shook her head. Resolve filled her face as she looked at Viola. "No," she said. "He wanted to keep me safe. He wanted to keep you safe. If he had made any mention of it, he would have worried about us. He knew what he was doing was dangerous." She paused to take a steadying breath. "Every day, I *wish* he would have confided in me. Maybe together we would have been able to work something out and he'd still be here."

As she spoke, Emilia's voice quietened. But it wasn't as wistful as Viola thought it would be. There was an edge to it. Maybe if her dad had been open to working with someone else, he wouldn't have had to give his life. It wasn't something she wanted to dwell on too much.

"It's not your fault, Mum."

"I know, but it doesn't make it feel any better." She stopped to look at Viola. "You're just like him. Stubborn, and refusing to do what's best for you. I see him in you, and sometimes I wish I couldn't."

Viola put her drink on the floor before moving over to her mum. "I will do whatever I can to make everyone safe, and I can't promise I won't put myself in danger. But I will try to stay safe."

Emilia pulled her into a tight hug. "Don't do anything stupid, Vi. What would I do if I lost you too?"

"Don't worry, Mum," she said as she stroked her mum's back.

****

Viola sat at her desk, running through the notes she had made earlier that day. Her concentration slipped as she felt compelled to fetch her phone from beneath the covers. Her usual idea of out of sight, out of mind was not working tonight, but she had a different reason for wanting to pick it up.

The conversation she'd had with her mum mulled over in her mind. She couldn't think of a reason why she should be doing this on her own, or why she was putting off making amends. With a sigh, Viola pushed herself away from her desk and collapsed onto her bed. She grabbed her phone from the pillow as she slid into bed.

I'm sorry for trying to do things on my own. Can we get past this and find a way to keep our families safe? Viola x

She put the phone back as she tried to sleep. She

couldn't promise to keep herself safe, but she would do whatever it took to keep everyone else safe if it was the last thing she did.

Chapter Sixteen

Viola shoved the notebooks back into the box. After the would-be revelation around the threading of energy, she hadn't been able to come across anything useful. She checked the group message. Still no response. She wanted to say something else. Anything to get them to respond, but she didn't want to push it. If they were that annoyed with her that they were refusing to respond after a couple of days, there was no need to make it worse. It hurt a little that William hadn't responded. He had seemed open to them all talking this through, but maybe he had spoken to Casey and changed his mind.

Even with the notebooks holding no trace of her dad's magic, she couldn't resist checking each of them over and over. But nothing. He had made sure to leave them clean of any tracing. It could have been his way of keeping what he was doing secret, but Viola couldn't help but wonder if this was another way to keep everyone else safe from what he had been practising.

She pushed her back against the edge of the bed. "I need to get out of this house. Do something without having to think about it."

An idea sprang into her mind. She picked up her phone and sent a short text to David. She jumped when her phone indicated a new message almost instantly.

"That was quick," she mumbled as she scanned the response. Her face picked up. "Looks like I won't be looking through all these books tonight after all."

****

"Are you sure you're not busy?"

"Too busy to help a damsel in distress? Never," David said, grinning at her.

"Don't you have a lot to do, being a business tycoon or whatever your job title is?"

"I do, but who wouldn't take time off to spend it with a feisty brunette?"

"Feisty?" Viola scoffed.

"I don't know many people who move from a crumpled heap to sassy defensiveness like you did."

"Touché."

Viola settled back into the leather sofa. She let the comfort and tranquillity of the moment descend over her. How easy would it be to stay here and forget about everyone else? Not that she would allow herself to do anything so selfish. Although, she was happy for any distractions.

"Why did you need to escape so suddenly?"

"It wasn't sudden."

"Really? You always want to be whisked away at nine p.m.?"

Viola cringed. "Okay, I needed to get out. Get away from my own thoughts. I thought you would be a good distraction."

"Is that all you see me as?" David asked. Viola admired the way his eyes crinkled at the corners as he spoke. "I can be a whole lot more than a distraction."

"I bet that's what you say to all the girls," Viola said as she took a sip of her water.

"Only those I find in crumpled heaps." He almost seemed to purr the words at her.

Maybe it was a bad idea to come here. In the soft glow of his living room, it didn't matter how much she knew this couldn't go anywhere. She rested her hand on his arm, the slight hum from the contact pulling her in. She drifted forward as she concentrated on his eyes. There was something there she couldn't quite read. It excited her more than she wanted to admit.

"I hope you don't find many women in that state," she said softly, inching closer to him.

"I could count the number of times it's happened on one hand." His face dipped slowly down to hers.

She could feel his breath on her cheeks; the gentle caress of intimacy pulled her closer. Her energy pulled her closer. Her eyes drifted shut. Anticipation bubbled through her body.

"David, how many times have I told you to keep that door locked?" A gruff voice broke the spell that surrounded them.

Viola scooted back across the sofa, her heart thudding in her chest. David cleared his throat, regret skipping across his face before he stood and turned towards the front of the house.

"Father, I didn't know you would be visiting this evening. How are you?"

An older man strode into the room. The resemblance between them was striking. She could see how David would age down to the lines dusted across his dad's face. Their eyes and jaw were almost identical. The only difference she could see was the emotions displayed on their faces. David was carefree, almost joyful, whereas harsh lines shaped his dad's. Viola was sure it wasn't only age to blame.

"When have you ever concerned yourself with my well-being?" His dad almost seemed to sneer. "I left you a message saying we had important affairs to discuss. Have you—" His gaze landed on Viola. She tried not to fidget under his stare. "I see you have a guest."

David sighed. "Father, this is Viola. Viola, this is my father, Matthew Richardson."

Viola scrambled to her feet, hand extended. "It's lovely to meet you."

Matthew regarded her hand but didn't take it. "By that I assume my son has not said much about me." He turned from her. "This is important, David, and here you are with any woman you can coax in."

Viola saw red. With more control than she realised she could wield, she kept a hold of the magic within, restraining its automatic attempt to defend her honour, but she couldn't stop herself from glaring at him. Matthew made no move to keep the contempt from his face. The tension in the room rose.

"David, Matthew. Where have you two boys gotten to?" A softer, quieter voice sounded through the room.

A small woman walked into the tense atmosphere. She glanced between the three of them, sadness reaching her eyes as she looked at Viola before she closed away the emotion.

"Hello, dear," she said, a smile radiating in her voice. "I'm David's mother, Rose."

"Viola," she said quietly.

"Why did you not tell us you had a guest round, David?" his mother scolded.

"I never got the message you were coming," he replied, his voice tight.

"No matter. Go speak with your father. I'm sure Viola here can keep me company."

David inclined his head slightly before turning towards Matthew. "Will the study be okay?"

He walked off, leaving Viola alone. This was not the break she had been hoping for.

****

"How long have you known David?" Rose asked Viola after they both settled back onto the sofa.

"A couple of months maybe."

"Oh."

Rose looked at her. The intensity of the gaze made Viola want to fidget.

"What do you do?" Rose asked.

"I'm sorry?"

"For work, dear."

"I'm a nurse in the local children's hospital. It's stressful," she added after a pause.

"How did you meet David?"

"He helped me." Viola stopped, not sure how

much to explain. "He found me in a heap outside one day. One small fainting spell, and a couple of week later, he literally ran into me. Well, more like jogged. We've stayed in touch since."

"He hasn't told me anything about you."

"We've not spent much time together, but he's been a good friend and someone to talk to."

"Friend?" Rose raised her eyebrow. Her body shifting slightly as she looked harder at Viola.

"Yeah, he's a good friend." Viola tried to ignore the look Rose was giving her. Did he not have many friends? It wasn't something she wanted to concentrate on after what had almost happened between them.

Viola cleared her throat. "Do you spend a lot of time with David?"

"Not as much as I would like," Rose admitted. "He doesn't make much time for us anymore. It upsets his father greatly."

"Is that why you're here tonight?"

"No. Matthew wanted to discuss something with him and hadn't been able to reach him via the phone."

"Oh."

Silence settled over them. Viola wanted to leave. Here she was at twenty-five and still not comfortable around someone else's parents. As she decided to make her excuses and leave, a noise sounded from down the hall.

"Excuse me, dear," Rose said, walking in the direction David had led his father.

"You've got your answer, and I won't be changing my mind. I think you should go." Viola heard the muted shout.

"How dare you speak to me in such a manner? You

will show me respect."

The conversation faded as whatever door had opened was closed on them. Viola sat locked in a tense, awkward silence that she wasn't sure how to leave. She picked up her previously discarded glass and finished the water. It stopped her fidgeting for a short time.

She made her way into the kitchen when a door slammed down the hall. She pulled her energy around her, trying to block out the noise. She wouldn't want anyone to hear her argue with her mum, and she could offer David a small piece of privacy. She counted to ten before letting the energy drop. Footsteps pattered down the wooden hallway.

"Viola?" David called.

"In the kitchen."

His silhouette framed the doorway. "I'm sorry you had to hear any of that." His hand ruffled his hair. "We've never had the best relationship."

"No need to apologise. Families can be a bit much." She smiled softly at him.

"About earlier—"

"I should go—"

They both started at once.

"You don't want to stay?" David asked.

Viola chewed the inside of her mouth. "I need to make sure I'm home in time for work tomorrow. I didn't realise how late it was when I came here."

"Okay," David responded, his body dropping. "I'll give you a lift back."

"No, it's fine. I can get a taxi."

"Viola, I'm not letting you pay for a taxi home. Come on. It won't take too long."

"Fine." She laughed. "I get the feeling you won't

take no for an answer on this."

As she moved to walk past him, David gently wrapped his fingers around her wrist and pulled her towards him. "Thank you," he whispered before lowering his head and brushing his lips against her cheek.

She shivered at his touch. "Wh-what for?"

"For being you." He smiled. A small blush rose across her face. "For not fighting me on this. I want to make sure you get home safe. You don't know what could happen out there." He brushed a strand of her hair from her face. "And for not judging my parents, or at least not passing judgement on them. I don't know what my mum put you through but thank you for staying with her."

"You're welcome."

Chapter Seventeen

"I'm glad you agreed to meet me," Viola said as the drinks were brought over to their table.

The café was quiet after the midday lunch rush. The hum of conversation was enough that they shouldn't be overheard, but it wasn't too loud as to distract them from each other.

"No need for you to offer such a formal invitation," William said, grabbing his cappuccino from the tray.

"Speak for yourself," Casey shot back.

"I know you didn't need to come, but I wanted to make any amends I could."

"A free coffee, or tea, isn't going to do that."

"I know, but I wanted us to have some neutral ground." She held the warm cup to her body. "I'm not what you think I am."

Casey started to speak when William prodded her.

"We agreed to come and hear her out, Case. The least we can do is let her speak without interruption."

"Fine." She folded her arms over her body and stared ahead of her, ignoring the drink in front of her.

"As I was saying, I'm not the person you think I am. I don't know why anyone thinks I am that way. I know I do what I want, but you have no idea what it's like to be known as Alex's daughter. I feel like I have this huge weight hanging over me. Everyone wondering what I will do, if I can live up to his legacy. So, I practised where I could. But that wasn't enough. It's felt like nothing I do is enough. I didn't stay away from anyone, but no one wanted to spend time with me. Tainted by association, maybe. I find it hard to trust others because I've never been given a reason to trust anyone. And when I told you what I knew, you blew up at me. How did you think that would help anything?"

Casey glared at Viola. Before she could speak, William touched her arm. "Thank you for letting us know that, Viola. It must be difficult for you."

"Yeah, really difficult." She huffed out. She picked up the peppermint tea and drank a small amount without looking towards Viola.

"Casey, you're not helping." William said. His tone was even and he turned his attention to Casey. "You agreed to help me with what I had planned to help the coven. If you can't put aside your own prejudices, then maybe you need to find someone else to help rather than stick with us."

"You're taking her side?"

"It's not about sides, Casey. It's about keeping all the people we love safe. If that's not important to you, then maybe it was a bad idea to involve you in this."

William kept his eyes on Casey. He wasn't angry that she was unwilling to accept Viola's apology, but he didn't seem happy with how she was behaving.

"Fine, whatever. I can be civil if we can find a way to keep everyone safe." Casey sat further back into her chair.

"Thank you, Will." Viola looked down at her drink. This was going to be harder than she initially thought.

"I'm talking to you too, Viola. We need to learn to work together if we want to get any of this to work."

She nodded at him, not trusting herself to say anything.

"Now, if we've all decided to at least a temporary truce, do we want to go over the bit you think you understand?"

****

Rain streaked down the bus window, unaware Viola had chosen a line she wanted to win. Would it make much of a difference? No, but it was better than thinking about their failures. She'd tried to find out when the protection might end, but there was nothing concrete. Why wouldn't her dad have made it obvious? If they knew, it would have given them more idea of how long they had left.

Something else bothered her about the notes. They were too cryptic. What was he hiding with the spell he'd created? Whatever it was, she hoped it would be important enough to keep hidden. Although it didn't make the process any less frustrating.

She pulled the current notebook from her rucksack. Wedging her knees into the chair in front, she laid the book on her makeshift desk. She skimmed the pages, willing something to jump out at her. It wasn't a tactic she had tried before, but she didn't hold much hope that this would work any better. It would take years to understand all the puzzles he'd left behind. Her fingers traced the pattern of the woven magic. There was something there she wasn't seeing. Casey and William hadn't had any different ideas either.

She rested a finger against the page as she used her other hand to flip through the book. The diagram had been sketched a few times, but none of the riddles matched up, and none of the understandable notes matched up to the first instance she'd noticed. Her thoughts wouldn't move from the pattern. She'd seen something similar when threading, but why would she need to make her own magic stronger? It didn't make any sense. Unless it wasn't only her magic that was supposed to be weaved.

She stilled. Was that it? Had William been right before? Her finger followed the diagram in front of her; the energy looked like it was coming from different points. She hit her face with the pages. She shouldn't have dismissed William's suggestion. If she hadn't been so pig-headed they could be a few weeks further along with solving the problem.

Viola peered at the page, but she couldn't tell how many people needed to join to make this work. Three would have to be enough. Something like joy bubbled through her. The feeling quickly deflated. They would need to trust each other a lot more than they currently did. They might have agreed to a truce, but it didn't mean they had dealt with any of the bigger issues between them. There was also a small passage next the diagram. It wasn't something that had been mentioned before, but if it was next to this, it had to be important. She grabbed her own notebook and quickly transferred the information.

Without thinking about it for too long, she grabbed her phone from her pocket. Her fingers glided across the screen as she typed up her thoughts. Casey couldn't ignore the importance of this. She sent the message asking for them to meet her.

She slid back into the seat. If she was right, someone else must have helped her dad. Someone in the coven would know what he did to keep them safe. They should still be alive. A gnawing fear slowly replaced her euphoria. If anyone else knew what had happened, why hadn't they spoken up? Why would they keep something a secret that would protect the coven? Protect themselves? Viola refused to believe her dad had been strong enough to go through with this plan on his own. If he had, he wouldn't have needed to work out combining energies between multiple people. No, someone else had to know.

"Please answer," she whispered to her phone.

She didn't know if the garbled message she sent would make any sense, but she hoped the urgency of her tone would make up for that. Three brains were better than one. If either of them could see where she was coming from, it might buy back some time. The time she'd wasted trying to do it on her own. Maybe Casey hadn't been wrong about her. If William hadn't asked her to help, would she have reached out to anyone? Viola grimaced. She knew the answer to that question, and it didn't make her feel better. If they were going to be a team, she needed to work out her issues and trust the others. Viola resolved to tell them the other pieces of her magic she'd been working on. The ones that didn't link to strengthening the protection. It could give them an advantage if nothing else.

Not knowing what else to do, she placed the book back into her bag. A headache would be her only prize if she let her mind wander over the pages for any longer. "There has to be something we're missing. Who would Dad have told?"

Her thoughts briefly landed on her mum. Unless she'd had her memory wiped, she couldn't imagine her mum had known any of the intricate details of what had been done. She'd already admitted as much. Who would leave their friends and families vulnerable if they had a way to keep them safe? No one sprang to mind. Not one person Viola could think of would let the protection languish.

The phone buzzed in her hand, distracting her from the spiral of her thoughts. She swiped across to her messages, relief falling over her.

Wait, wait, wait. You're telling me those squiggles ARE magic?!

I know, I should have listened to you before. Vi x

If we could find anyone else who knows what happened, we could crack this wide open! W

I am a little ashamed that I brushed it off. I guess that's my dad for you. Vi x

Have you asked anyone about this? Casey.

No, I wanted to let you know first. Do you think anyone would answer us? Vi x

If they do, they might be too scared to do anything to help. I'll start asking around. It might push someone to slip up and give us something to work with. Casey.

Viola wedged her phone into her pocket. If nothing else, this had removed the frosty undertone to their messages. She cleared her mind as she prepared to face another day at work.

****

The wind bit at Viola's face as she left the building. It was unusually cold for a summer night. She followed her path to the bus stop on autopilot. As she left the hospital, and its signal-defying coating, she'd fired a text to Casey and William. What better time to test out their theory? They could also make a list of her dad's potential accomplices. It might be that no one would talk after keeping quiet for twenty years, but it was a step in the right direction. She might have to put her mum under the spotlight.

From her previous experience with the rest of the coven, Viola wasn't expecting the answers to fall into her lap. It would have been too easy if her mum knew what needed to be done. Maybe easy wasn't the right word, but surely, she wouldn't have let the coven get this close to the edge if she knew. She didn't think they necessarily needed to find the helpers and convince them to help. She needed to know if what they *knew* could help. A small push in the right direction was all she wanted now. Even confirmation of her thoughts would be enough.

As she waited for her bus, the icy cold that swirled around her was replaced with an uncomfortable sensation oozing over her. She was reminded of the incident a few weeks before. It was the same feeling of dread and fear that crept through her body. Her already puckered skin tingled more. It wasn't something she thought she would experience again, especially not out in the open.

Had someone left a piece of magic to track her out here? Her eyes darted around, examining the dark spaces in front of her. Nothing was out of place, or at least nothing jumped out at her. Viola tried to pinpoint the signature, tried to pick up on the magic closing in around her. Maybe it wasn't something left over. Maybe it was someone nearby.

Viola steadied her mind and took a deep breath. Her nerves wouldn't settle. She flexed her fingers and hoped it would be enough for her to focus. She let her mind drift into the uncomfortable sensation of being watched. She gasped. The opposing energy swamped her senses, her focus almost lost. She braced herself against the feeling as she gathered her thoughts. Her face scrunched as she focused, forcing her own energy into a weak spot of the one threatening to pull her under.

As the minutes ticked by, her frustration grew. The dread had been building slowly within her. Every second she let her energy search was a second she left herself exposed. She took a shaky breath, ignoring the mist that sprang from her mouth. Another thirty seconds; that was all she could give herself. She felt the faint ghosting over her skin, pushing and testing against the intruding feelings.

Hope had almost left her when she felt something. A flicker of joy passed through her as she concentrated on the spot. It was small and almost hidden. If she didn't practice tracing energy often, she might have missed it. Not for the first time, Viola thanked her mum for letting her practise when she wanted. She used a tendril of energy to tease at the spot, pulling at the imperfection until it frayed and tattered. A small squeak passed through her lips as she realised what she'd managed. Before she could go further, she retreated and pulled her energy back to her. If she broke it completely, they would know what she was, a risk she wouldn't allow to follow her to the rest of the coven.

Viola sucked in air through clenched teeth as she covered her mind from any dread. Her body was tense, but she didn't know if it was the power she had used or the cold around her. How long would it be before whoever was trying to catch her succeeded?

****

"This has happened before?" William asked her after she finished explaining the latest strange experience. Viola was thankful that he didn't say anything about her keeping the previous experience to herself. She was glad that someone else was taking her seriously, and saw it for the threat she believed it to be.

"A few weeks ago." Viola nodded, draping herself over the kitchen chair. "Something happened at the hospital. It wasn't a lot, but it felt like someone was watching me. Like they knew who I was but wanted to make sure. Baiting me."

"Or they knew someone in the hospital was a witch but needed to confirm who it was," William suggested. "Although, if they went for you at the bus stop, I'm guessing they have a pretty good feeling."

"I know. I'm worried. We need to figure out what my dad did, and quickly. I don't want to be the one who couldn't help, and who might have led a witch hunter to the coven." She leaned forward against the table. "I still don't get how no one would come forward with what he did."

William shrugged. "Could be they're scared of whatever happened to your dad. Don't want to follow in his footsteps."

"They want someone else to do it instead?"

"Or they don't want anyone to."

Viola narrowed her eyes at him. "What do you mean? The coven is always talking about strengthening the protection spell. Why would they talk about that without wanting anyone to go through with it?"

"If you could strengthen the magic without starting over, wouldn't you do that?" He held up his hand. "No, I haven't heard anything before you start. But it would make sense with what's happening. If they can find where the spell has been concentrated, they might be able to understand just enough to feed into it, rather than go through everything."

"Why do you always have some logical reasoning for my ideas?" She sighed dramatically at him. "Maybe I should have continued this as a solo mission."

William laughed. "Casey and I are here to rein you

in. Can't let Miss Everett run off with another one of her hare-brained ideas." His face turned serious. "It makes sense, though. Why are they so adamant on finding out where your dad was at the end? That way, they might be able to retrace his steps."

"Eurgh, I wish I knew what happened that night. There's nothing in the notebooks saying where this was meant to happen. Or maybe there is, and we haven't figured it out yet. There's only one thing I've found that's hinted at a time, but it's more like a day in the month. But it doesn't say which month. I feel like we're running into a wall." Her words muddled as she pressed her head further into the table.

"We'll get there eventually." He reached over to squeeze her arm to reassure her. "Before the protection vanishes completely if we're lucky."

Viola pushed herself upright. "Do you know if Casey has had much luck with it all?"

"Probably not."

"Have you spoken to her? She still doesn't seem too willing to talk to me."

"Yeah, we talk." He paused. "Have you tried talking to her directly? Outside of the group chat, or in person?"

Viola shook her head.

"You could try. I think you're both too stubborn to give in. Make the first move."

"But I've already apologised. Can't we move past this?"

"Try again."

Viola stared at him. His gaze was unflinching from her pout. She sighed. "Fine, o' wise William. I'll see if she will answer a phone call later. Or show up at her door."

"Any time. I can fix any problems you may be having."

"Thanks." She grinned. "But if we could focus on the notebooks, that would be great."

****

"Here goes nothing," Viola said as she rapped at the door in front of her.

She tapped her foot as she waited. If she was lucky, she wouldn't be standing outside for long. Not that she had much luck. After an almost endless wait, the sound of the handle turning broke her solitude.

"What are you doing here?" Casey asked her. She stood in the gap the door had opened up, not allowing any space for Viola to come in.

"We need to talk." Viola tried to keep the pleading tone from her voice.

"I don't think we do." Casey started to close the door.

"Please."

Casey sighed and moved to let Viola enter.

"Thanks."

"Yeah, whatever," Casey muttered under her breath.

Casey showed her to the living room. Viola perched on the edge of her chair. Silence deafened them. Casey stared at her, the warm brown eyes burning into her own.

"So, talk."

"I wanted to apologise. I didn't know what was happening in the coven around me, and it's no excuse.

I shouldn't have made out that anyone could have done what I do without reprimand. To be honest, I thought I was being sneaky with my magic. I never realised you all knew, and that you were all talking about me." Viola rushed through her speech. "I wanted to do what I could to make my dad proud, and I had no idea how to do it. It never made sense to me that he risked his life for us to be safe, and then not do what we can to make the world a better place. Why would he want to sacrifice himself for us to still hide? It was childish, and I'm sorry."

She dropped her gaze, not wanting to know what Casey would do.

"Okay," Casey said.

Her head shot up. "Okay?"

"Okay."

Viola looked at her. "Look, I know I've always been a bit on the loner side. But I need you and Will."

"I get it. When do we next need to meet up?"

"Whenever." Viola paused. "Unless you've made any headway with the notebooks or finding out who might know anything about how more than one person would have had to be involved for the protection to work."

"No. What was with your dad? No offence. But who was he hiding his work from?"

She shrugged. "Honestly, I wish I knew. At least I could go pester them instead of you and Will."

Casey smiled slightly at that. "I don't know if I'd wish that on anyone."

"And here I thought we were becoming friends."

"Hmm, maybe at least friendly acquaintances."

"Does that mean you're willing to help perform the

magic?"

Casey looked pensive. "Of course. You shouldn't doubt me trying to help with that."

Chapter Eighteen

Viola lounged across the sofa. For the past thirty minutes, she had been psyching herself up to talk to her mum. She didn't usually feel this way, this on edge.

"Who were Dad's friends?"

Emilia peered at her daughter over the edge of her book. "Why do you want to know?"

"I'm just curious."

"You're never *just* anything, Viola. What are you scheming?"

"I'm scheming nothing. I want to know who he might have spoken to about his experiments."

"If he never spoke to me about them, what makes you think he spoke to anyone else?"

"A hunch I have."

Emilia sighed. "There were a few people he spent time with, but most of them moved to other covens after his death. They didn't agree with the way he was left to struggle through this on his own."

"Some of them stayed?"

"Yes, Viola. Some of them stayed. But I don't know if any of them would want to talk about it."

Viola sat quietly, her mind going through the people who had been nicest to her. "This would be a lot easier if you'd help me."

"That might be true, but won't it feel better knowing you've managed it on your own?"

"No. I'm trying to save people, not finish a crossword." She moved into an upright position, pushing away from her mum.

"I know, Vi. I know. But I don't know what you want me to tell you. When your dad died, I tried to find out whatever I could. No one would speak to me. I don't know if they didn't know, or if they were guilty that they couldn't stop him from leaving us behind."

"But he must have had friends."

"He did, a lot of them. But I can't see them helping you any more than they helped me."

Viola huffed and pushed herself from the chair.

"Where are you going?"

"To see if I can pester anyone else to help me."

Emilia shook her head. "Don't alienate yourself further from the coven."

"I'll try not to."

****

Viola had no plan. The only person she could think to ask about her dad was Ms. Glorian, and she already knew what her thoughts were on that. There hadn't been a meeting scheduled for a couple of weeks, which left her with no choice but to head to the local community centre. With her days off being few and far between, she wouldn't usually spend time helping out, but some of the older members of the coven volunteered their time.

She pressed her fingers against the peeling paint of the sun-bleached door, exhaled, and pushed the wooden entrance open. There was no quieting of the voices. No immediate stop to stare at what she was doing there. She blended into the background as she tried to remember the names of the coven members she could see dotted around the room.

A familiar face stood behind the refreshment table.

"Viola, I didn't expect to see you at one of these." Charlotte raised an eyebrow at her.

"I wanted to do something to help out the local community."

Charlotte made a noise, indicating she didn't believe anything she had to say. "If you want to help, you can clear up some of the mess left about the room. The centre management is keen for us to keep the place as tidy as it was when our hours started."

"You can count on me." Viola turned to leave.

"Don't cause any trouble."

"I'm not here to do that."

"You may not be here with that purpose, Viola Everett, but you wouldn't be here unless you had some other plans."

"I promise not to cause any issues with the group you run."

Charlotte shooed her on.

Viola made her way to the outer edges of the tables to pick up the discarded paper plates and cups. She didn't have anything to put them in and spent the first half an hour walking back and forth to the small bin in the corner of the room. The other coven members gathered in the room gave her a small greeting, but none of them started a conversation with her. It was times like this when she wished she'd not isolated herself so much from the rest of them.

As she finished her hundredth circle of the room, one of the coven members beckoned her over.

"Viola, what are you doing here?"

"What I can to help the community, Ben."

"You tell lies as well as your father did. What's your real reason for being here?"

Viola flopped into the chair nearest him. "I'm trying to find someone who can help me with what my dad might have been up to. I thought I might run into someone here who could help."

"Should have known it would be about Alex. You don't have to live up to his memory, you know."

"I know, but I want to try."

Ben shook his head. "No one here can help you. Your dad wasn't as much of a recluse as you've tended to be, but he didn't make everyone his confidant."

"Do you know who might have been?"

"There were a few who were closer to him than others, but there's no guarantee. Are you sure this is something you want to do?"

Viola nodded, the risks never far from her mind. "Please, Ben."

"There's no diverting once an Everett sets their mind on something." Ben settled into the plastic chair. "There's a couple of vocal members of the coven; you might have heard them in the meetings. They were some of Alex's closest friends. They would be your best options to get any information he passed on."

"The vocal members? That's not very helpful information."

"Some people wouldn't be so picky about the help they got."

"Sorry. I feel like I'm floundering. I'm not at my best at the moment. Thanks for the help."

"You're welcome. Someone needed to do something to help. Don't let them stop you from what you're doing. We've hidden away for so long that people have forgotten what it's like to do what needs to be done."

Viola scooped up her bag, but before she left, she headed back to Charlotte. "Thank you for letting me stay. I've cleaned up what I could find, and I hope it helps to keep the place tidy before you finish."

"It should be sufficient. If you feel like being helpful in future, we'd always welcome the extra hands."

"If there's a place in my schedule, I will see what I can do."

Chapter Nineteen

Viola sat at her desk, mulling over her notebook. She flipped back to the notes she had made earlier in the week. There were the notes on the weaving; it almost looked like the energies had been plaited. If she could find a way to utilise all three of them, she might be able to channel strength into the protection. She grabbed a green coloured pen from the pot on her desk to make additional notes. She wasn't convinced the different colours helped her to understand any better, but it was a habit she had kept since her studies.

She re-wrote the little phrase that had been near the image. The words hadn't meant too much to her before, but it felt like there was something there. She hadn't been lying to William when she said she didn't have any concrete information, but this phrase mentioned the *darkest night*. To her, that could only be a new moon, but she wanted to make sure there weren't any other times it could refer to.

Viola picked up her phone and looked for anything that 'darkest night' could refer to. She wrote down anything that was flagged, but the majority of what she could find was related to various films and games that had been named this. She hoped her dad hadn't been referring to some sort of horror franchise. She chuckled to herself at the thought. That would be something unexpected by everyone in the coven.

While the phone was in her hand, she flicked to her contacts and pulled up William's information. He might have more of an idea of what it could mean.

"Hello?" he answered after the first ring.

"No need to sound so confused."

"You don't make it a habit to contact people, and then you start phoning them. What is wrong with you, Vi?"

She could hear him laughing at her. "I've found something that could be something or nothing. But I can't get my head to work on it."

"Aww, and you chose me to rubber duck with. I am flattered."

"You know what, I might have made a mistake. I'll phone Casey instead."

"No, no, no. Wait, I can help you. What is it?"

Viola sighed. "If someone said darkest night to you, what would that mean to you?"

"Hmm, no other context? It could be the solstice, or a new moon. Or it could be a night where everything goes wrong, but I don't know how you'd know that."

"I was thinking a new moon, but the internet suggested horror themed things. I never thought it could be the solstice. That's too far away." Viola's voice trailed off as she finished.

"Do we need to brainstorm this in person?"

"Maybe."

"Okay, I'll get in touch with Casey. Tell us where you want us to meet, and we'll be there."

"Thanks, Will."

"No problem. That's what we're here for."

Viola smiled as she hung up the phone. This might be easier than they thought.

****

Viola shivered as the wind blew through the trees around them. The twilight light dappled through the branches and created a kaleidoscope of patterns on the floor. She turned to Casey and William, who had taken up space on some neighbouring rocks.

"Why do you love being out here?" Casey asked as she pulled her jacket close around her front.

"It's quiet and you can practise without worrying about being stumbled on." Viola had turned her attention back to the notebook in her hand.

"No one stumbled across you at Padley Gorge?"

"Do you see anyone else here?" Viola ignored the scoff in Casey's voice.

"Timing might be everything," William mused. "Sure, a Saturday or Sunday mid-morning might be busy but who comes out on a Thursday evening? No one was on the other side when we first tried seeing how to get the energies to recognise each other."

"Exactly. Thank you, William," Viola murmured in agreement. Her finger skimmed down the page until it reached the passage she'd noted down. "Any ideas on how we need to do this?"

William shook his head. "No instructions?"

Viola grimaced. "No. Dad didn't make any of this easy."

"What's the worst that could happen?" William asked as he moved closer to look at the page.

"We cause a power overwhelm and die." Casey looked between them. "If we don't know what we're doing, is it safe? If we kill ourselves, we'll never be able to help everyone else."

Viola steeled herself and took a long, slow breath. She knew Casey was only being cautious, but she was struggling with this new dynamic between them. When this was all over, maybe they would be able to work towards a real friendship.

"What does it say?" William asked before Viola had the chance to respond.

She cleared her throat. "*On the darkest night of the month, funnel the magic and strengthen the bond. All held within the link protect and hide.*" Viola finished and looked at her two companions.

"So, the darkest night could be a new moon," Casey mused. "Although, I guess it could be the solstice; it would be more impactful. And everyone who is linked to the coven is safe. It sounds like it should be something straightforward."

"It should be, but he didn't say how the magic sticks or why it would wear away over time."

"But it's enough to start with," William said. "We need to channel the energy into protecting everyone. Shall we hold hands and try that?"

Viola shrugged. "We may as well try it. I feel like we're missing something, though."

All three of them moved closer together. Viola grabbed a hold of both Casey and William. She concentrated on the feeling she wanted to work through her energy. Protection was something that she had threaded into her home when she wanted to stop people from intruding. It seemed a little crude compared to keeping the coven hidden from someone who wanted to harm them.

She felt out for their individual energy signatures. They were easy to find and call to her after having spent some time getting used to them, though she doubted that they would feel as familiar to her as her mum. She tried to link the three of them together in their goal to protect. Her concentration slipped, as did her grasp on what they were doing.

"It doesn't appear to have worked." Casey let go of Viola's hand. "If we don't have anywhere to keep the magic, we won't be able to create the protection."

"I know," Viola said as she rubbed her head. "I tried to weave our energies together, but they didn't want to stay together. Maybe we need to find a way to make our energies more in sync."

"Do you have any ideas of what that could be?" William asked.

Viola shook her head. "Not unless the weaving is something more permanent."

Casey gasped. "It could be a joining. But I don't know of anyone taking part in one. It's something Abigail doesn't like talking about."

"Let's look into that with more detail and see if we can figure out how the joining works and why it's frowned on," William said.

"Okay, can you two look into that?" Viola asked as

she leaned back against the closest rock. "I have an idea of how to get the protection in place, but I might need a little more time to look into it. It would work better if we have something to anchor it to. Do either of you know of anything that is a permanent link to the coven's magic?"

William shook his head. "I've never been told of anything since I moved here."

"I don't know of anything either. I can't remember anyone talking about a symbol for the coven, but I might have forgotten. We should be able to ask around, though," Casey said.

Viola rubbed her eyes. "I think that should be the next thing we work on, then. If we've not managed to do anything today, then we need to find out where we can anchor this to on the next New Moon." She opened her phone. "It looks like we missed the last one by a couple of days."

"Why has nothing about this gone easily yet?" William asked. He ran his hands through his hair and looked at the sky. "Just once, Alex, we could have done with something straightforward."

"Because then it wouldn't have been something we needed to try and resolve," Viola said with a wry smile. "But it gives us some time to find out where we need to link this."

"I'll ask Abigail if she has any ideas and let you both know," Casey said. She rubbed her hands together. "Now, if we've exhausted our chances tonight, can we go home and warm up?"

"Sure. I'll give you a lift," William said.

Chapter Twenty

"Oh, Viola, thank goodness," Emilia said as Viola entered the house.

"Mum, what's up?"

"Someone else has gone missing. And then you didn't answer your phone —"

"What do you mean?"

"Someone from our coven has gone missing. Ms. Glorian is beside herself with worry. When she first issued out the notice, she didn't say who it was, and then when she did, I worried you'd been taken as well."

"Who's gone?"

"Evie. She's been missing for about twelve hours. It's unlike her. She usually stays in contact with a number of people through the day, so we know something has happened."

"Slow down. Do we need to worry about this? Are we sure that she's *missing* missing?"

Emilia glared at Viola.

"I'm not saying we shouldn't, but is it something we should panic over?" Viola placed her coat over the closest chair.

"We should always worry when one of our own goes missing. It doesn't matter who it is, or why they're gone. Would you want people to ignore it if it was you who had gone missing?"

"I bet they would anyway," Viola muttered.

"I heard that," Emilia said, moving from the living room. "What about William and Casey? They've been spending a lot of time with you."

"It's not been by choice. We need each other for-" Viola caught herself, but not soon enough.

"For what?"

The look Emilia gave her was one she knew too well. She shuffled nervously to her other foot. Was there anything she could say that would help her get out of this one? With a sigh, she looked up to the ceiling.

"Some magic we've been working on."

"Your dad's notebooks?"

Viola nodded and ventured a look towards her mum. "I couldn't figure them out myself, and William thought we might be able to manage something if we worked together."

"Has it worked?"

"I guess it depends on when this person was taken, but no. I don't think it is working. We've tried everything we can, but half of Dad's notes don't make any sense. And I'm trying so hard to make sure that I don't mess this up," Viola admitted. "I don't want people to keep looking at me like there's something wrong with me."

"What do you mean?"

"Everyone has always treated me differently. No one wanted to spend time with me, and Casey confirmed that it was something that people actively did. They see me as some sort of upstart who's trying to overthrow Ms. Glorian. Why would I want that responsibility? But I'm hoping doing something to help the coven will help change some people's minds."

"Viola, if you want to prove the coven wrong, you need to show her you aren't what they say. Don't stress out about it too much." Emilia turned to leave. "Maybe you can convince her sooner than you thought."

"Why? What's happening?"

"We need to head to Ms. Glorian's house. She wants to discuss some new measures in light of this recent disappearance."

****

Chairs were littered around the small space, the gaps between them so small you wouldn't be able to put your legs anywhere comfortably. The coven sardined themselves into any available gap between the furniture. Viola opted to stand, keeping her back against the wall and as far away from anyone as she could. Casey and William were there. She half went to them, but she wasn't sure if they would want her sitting with them. She stayed close to her mum and looked over the room.

She thought about what they had been doing that evening. It seemed unlikely that they would have been trying to put the protection in place before anything happened, so it could have still worked. Not that she was keeping her fingers crossed on that. She made a note to ask about the time they might have gone missing. She let her thoughts die down as Ms. Glorian moved to the front of the room.

"I'm sure you've all heard the terrible news. Evie has been out of contact for the past thirteen hours. We are assuming the worst and believe this is linked to the still missing woman from the High Peak Coven. She has not yet been located, but we believe both to have involved witch hunters." She paused to allow the buzz from the room to quieten. "In light of this, the Elders, including myself, have decided to impose a strict set of rules."

Viola stared, her blood rushing through her ears. She forced small breaths from her body as the coven elder listed the new restrictions.

"Firstly, no witch is to use their magic outside of their own homes. Anyone caught doing this will be stripped from the coven's protection, as well as expelled from the coven. We will not let any one person be the downfall of us all."

Viola refused to look towards Casey and William.

"Secondly, we are imposing a curfew. No one is to be out after ten p.m., unless returning from their place of work. We are unaware of the circumstances of these disappearances, but we would like to mitigate this wherever possible. These rules will come into effect immediately. Any new rules will be instructed as soon as these have been decided."

"This is bullshit, and you know it, Abigail."

"Thomas, we've already had this discussion."

"No, you've talked at us. Do you believe the way to

keep us safe is to hide away and pretend that we're normal? If that's the best the Elders can come up with, it might be better to be on your own. At least then we won't have this policing of behaviours."

Viola stared at him. It wasn't often someone called out Ms. Glorian and not usually more than once in one sitting. She made a note to find him after the meeting. He might have been one of the people Ben had been hinting at.

"I know emotions are running high, but we are doing everything we can to keep everyone safe. You can speak to me privately if you have any serious concerns."

Thomas didn't say anything else, but Viola could feel his energy rippling out from him.

"If anyone has any concerns, please speak to me and we can run through anything that's on your mind."

Ms. Glorian stood, waiting for the questions and queries the coven members had. A few stood to talk to her privately. Viola remained against the wall. Heat rushed to her cheeks. Her energy wrapped around her as she tried to remain calm. A suspected witch hunter was kidnapping coven members and the only response the Elders had was to limit everyone's use of magic, and to limit their freedoms. *Typical.* At least someone was willing to say what circled in her mind, and it didn't look like he was being reprimanded in the way she knew she would be for the same response.

She forced her face to remain neutral. This was something she knew the Elders would be watching for. They knew she was helping the patients in the hospital. If she wanted to keep up her practice, she would have to find another way to keep everyone safe.

Viola left the house with her thoughts still fixed on finding Thomas when she felt something tapping at her energy. She staggered back a step and tried to press on, but it tapped again. When had they learnt to do something like that? She rubbed at her eyes.

"Fine," she muttered. "Let's get this over with."

She turned back and almost walked directly into William as she rounded the corner.

"I'm glad you listened to that." He smiled at her. "I'm still not sure what I did, but at least it worked."

"It was hard to ignore," she said.

"I was hoping that would be the case, but I'm not as adept at all this as you."

Viola sighed. "What is it?"

"Do you think Thomas might be one of the people we should speak to about what your dad was up to? He doesn't seem to agree with the rules that have been put in place."

"I had the same thought, but I don't know much about him, and I don't want to blindside him without anything important to ask."

They stood in silence for a few seconds before William spoke again. "I don't know if we failed, but I think we need to make sure it's in place."

Viola nodded. "To be honest, it didn't feel like anything had happened. Maybe we need to do something more than weave the energies together to push the protection in."

"Wait," William said. "You wove the energies together, but what if it's not the energies?" A strange look came over his face.

"What are you saying?"

"What if it's us that need weaving together and

then the energy will already be interlocked. You wouldn't need to do anything additional while putting the protection in place."

"I can't believe you're suggesting this."

"I can't believe you aren't." William smirked at her.

"We'll never get Casey to agree to this." Viola rubbed at her face.

"Don't underestimate her want to keep this coven safe. Plus, I think she's warming up to you."

"Do you not want to at least ask her about this?"

"No. I think you two need to put your big girl pants on and talk together and get over whatever it is that is between you."

Viola sighed. "Fine, do you know where she is?"

"I think she stayed back in the house to help clean up, but if not, she will have gone home."

"I'll check, but I might have to leave it until tomorrow." Viola pulled her phone from her pocket. "Half past nine. There's not enough time to get to her house and then be at home. Don't want to break the curfew on the first night."

"I didn't think you would be listening to that." This time, when William smiled, his eyes shone as well. "Text me when everything's sorted. We can practise at each other's houses and figure out a way to keep everyone protected. I doubt even the Elders could argue that's outside the rules."

✼✼✼✼✼✼✼✼✼✼✼✼✼

Viola headed back to Ms. Glorian's house to check if Casey was still there. She didn't attempt to try what William had done as she wasn't sure if it was something that could send a message back.

The front door stood ajar as stragglers trailed into the dark. Viola headed back to the main meeting area. Casey stacked chairs into a corner as a few other coven members spoke to Ms. Glorian. Viola inclined her head to the Elder before heading to the other side of the room.

"Hey, Casey," she said as she approached the other woman. "Do you have a minute?"

"Not really, but if you want to help, I can try and pay attention."

Viola started rearranging some of the furniture as Casey moved the extra chairs out of the way. "William has come up with an idea, that I think we might want to try."

"What is it?" Casey huffed as she pulled a table to the middle of the room.

Viola looked to make sure no one was close to them. "Maybe we need to weave more than the energy together."

Casey stopped, her eyes wide. "Are you suggesting what I think you are?" she whisper-shouted at her.

Viola winced but nodded. "He thinks it will be the best way to strengthen our energies and get the protection to stick in place."

Casey pushed her palms to the side of her head. "He would think that. We need to talk about this somewhere we have some privacy." She pulled her phone from her jacket pocket. "But not tonight. You both should come to mine tomorrow. I will let William know. I can't believe he would suggest something like this," she muttered to herself as Viola quickly left.

What were they getting themselves into?

Chapter Twenty-One

"Glad you were able to get Casey to agree to this. I knew you had it in you," William said to Viola as Casey let him into the house.

"I'm not sure if it was outright agreeing," Viola said as Casey rolled her eyes.

"What's the plan?"

The two women quickly looked at each other before Casey spoke. "Hopefully, we find a way to join our magics."

"Do we know any of the side effects? What might happen if we do this?"

Viola shook her head. "Unless either of you have figured out anything, I haven't seen anything."

Casey pinched her nose. "Okay, we might as well try this before I back out. What do we need to do?"

"I might have already done that. Tried it on my own, I mean. Don't look at me like that," she said to them. "I thought it was something to do with your own magic. I pulled the energy into three threads and kind of wove them into a similar pattern that was drawn. It felt stronger, but I couldn't understand why you'd want to do something like that."

"We need to weave our energies together, and then when we place the protection, it will be stronger?" William asked.

"I think so. But maybe we need to do it in a circle. Or a triangle, to keep all of us joined."

"Abigail is going to kill us if she finds out what we've done," Casey mumbled.

"Ms. Glorian can think what she likes. I haven't seen her come up with an idea to keep us all safe."

"You know if she finds out, it won't end well."

"Blame it on me. I'm sure she already dislikes me. It shouldn't take much to convince her I'm the root of the problem." Viola stopped and looked around the house. "Is this place secure?"

Casey narrowed her eyes. "What do you mean secure?"

"Warded? Protected?"

"No. I didn't know you could do that."

"May I?"

Casey nodded. Viola took a deep breath and placed minor protections around the room. Only small things, but it would stop anyone from stumbling across what they were attempting. Viola's body sagged as she added the final touches.

"Can you show me that?"

"Of course. I've only done it around the living room for now. We can try practising in a different room later."

"Thanks."

"Are we ready to try this?" William asked.

Viola nodded. She stilled herself, her breathing dictating her every move. She fell into the meditation. Her energy lapped around her, its warmth flooding her body. If she pressed gently, she could feel the world moving and living in the space in front of her. She focused her energy into tendrils wisping their way towards Casey and William. Before her energy could move across them, she could feel the faintest hint of theirs trying to reach her. The sudden caressing of their energies broke her concentration.

She shuddered. Was this why Ms. Glorian hadn't wanted to attempt this? It felt as though she was being exposed to the other two. She didn't realise opening up so much would cause such an effect. *It's only the energy, not my mind*, she thought, mantra-like, as she forced herself to concentrate.

"I don't think I will ever get used to that feeling," William said, breaking her concentration completely.

"I get what you mean. It feels far too vulnerable. Too intimate." Viola shuddered. Both nodded at her words. "I guess we know why they didn't want us practising this."

"Should we stop?" Casey asked.

"No," William said, suddenly serious. "We don't have time to give up. How long until the protection lowers? Or someone else is taken from another coven? Or even worse." He trailed off, not wanting to put words to the possibility.

"You're right." Viola sighed.

Casey straightened her back, pushing herself away from the back of the sofa. Her eyes hardened. "For the coven."

"For the coven," Viola and William echoed.

The trio moved closer to each other, grasping each other's hands and completing their triangle. As they sat around the small side table, she could feel their energies running across her palms. She was sure they could feel hers as well. This time, she was prepared for it. Her only comfort came from the familiar hum that tingled along her arms, lapping at the entwined fingers in each hand. She lowered the barriers around her body, the ones usually in place to trace any signs of danger. As they slowly descended, she could almost touch the energy from the other two witches in the room.

Their energies washed over her, searching for a way to entangle with her own. There was a discomfort to the feeling. One she hadn't been expecting. She fought against the nausea. She fought against the panic bubbling inside her. They didn't have time to wait to try this again. If they wanted to strengthen not only their coven but those near them, they needed to see this through. As quickly as it started, the feeling ended.

"Did it work?" William asked.

"I don't know. Do you feel any different?" Viola asked them.

"I never want to do that again," Casey said. She shook out the tension in her arms. "That was worse than when you gave me the electric shock. But I think it might have worked. I don't feel like I normally do. There's something else." She looked at Viola. "Did you manage to figure out anything to say how you know it's worked?"

"There was something underneath it all, but I'd need to double check if there's anything that makes sense. I think it was only a riddle, but not a clear one."

Viola flicked through the book she'd been carrying around with her, turning to the page detailing the magic.

"*Now as one, one is all. Power at your fingers climb. Lion's strength keeps strong.*"

She read aloud from the page, then looked at Casey and William. "I'm not sure what that last line might reference."

"Me neither," Casey admitted. "But it should mean we're stronger."

"We can try and see," Viola suggested. "Who wants to volunteer?"

"What have we got to lose?" William said as he stood, stretching out his arms and legs.

"Try moving the cushion on the chair," Casey said.

"Okay." William turned his attention to the small, blue cushion.

He took a deep breath, and suddenly, a zap filled Viola's body. The hairs on her arms stood on edge. A slight chill flashed down her spine. She glanced at Casey. The shock was reflected on the other woman's face. All three watched as the cushion slowly moved from the chair.

"Does it always feel like that?" Viola asked.

Casey shook her head. "I've never felt it so strong before."

"What happened?" William asked.

"We could feel your magic. The weaving must have worked," Casey said. "Now, we need to make this work for the coven."

Chapter Twenty-Two

"Why won't this work?" Viola asked. The cup at her side was still in two pieces.

Since she had combined her magic with Casey and William, she struggled to complete the simplest of tasks. Her drink had fallen from her desk, shattering the cup. Her own magic wasn't mending the pieces, not to mention the potential hack she'd stumbled upon.

It had been almost a week since they had joined, but she hadn't noticed anything from the others. Did they use their own so infrequently it hadn't caused an issue? Or was this a hint that all three were suffering?

Hey, have you two tried to do anything since the other night?

She needed to know it wasn't only her suffering from this. Anything to say this was normal would help the transition. Not that she wanted to have a limiter placed on herself. She cursed her dad again. If his notes made more sense, if they could decipher what he'd done, they wouldn't be here, struggling to do the most basic of tasks.

Her phone buzzed beside her.

Like what? W

Anything.

She took his response as a no. It made no sense to her that they were a coven who didn't practise. Could you be a coven if none of the members used their magic frequently?

"Well, there's no point sitting here," she said, brushing the flecks of pottery from her jeans.

She grabbed the two parts of the cup and dropped them into the bin. Leaving her room, she tucked her recent notebook under her arm as she made her way downstairs. Some time outside was in order. It might not clear her mind enough to understand what her dad had been talking about, but the fresh air would at least stop her from falling asleep.

The garden chairs were pushed against the patio wall, draining away the last remnants of the rainwater from the night before. Viola pulled a chair from the cool of the shade into the centre of the garden, chasing the sun to find its warmest part. She flipped the notebook open to the folded down corner as she perched on the edge of the plastic. Her focus rested on the entwined symbol. It was drawn across a few pages. Some had more dotted lines than others, but she couldn't see anything to explain what happened after. She looked around the pages to see if she could see anything that stood out. It was like playing the world's worst spot-the-difference game.

Her phone buzzed again.

Nope, no magic for me. I thought I'd felt a few things this week, though. Guess that was you? :) W

Sorry. I'm not used to not using it.

Nothing from me. I don't have a need for it day-to-day. Casey.

How can you not? Feeling the flow of it through your body. Doing something extraordinary. It's the best!

We'll leave that to you =D W

Viola smiled. The relationship between the three of them had been improving over the past week. It wasn't quite a friendship, but the messages didn't feel as forced as they had before. Even Casey's frostiness didn't hold the bite it had. It was a step in the right direction. Having other people to help her through this hadn't been as much of a chore as she'd expected. If only they brought some understanding on her magic's lessening potency.

****

Viola led the other two into her room. She made sure

to turn up the heat to combat the cold of the air that had drifted into the house as they arrived.

"Why didn't we do this to start with?" Casey asked.

"I try not to do too much magic at home. Don't ask. I think I was hiding it from my mum when I was younger, and it became a habit."

"What's the plan?" William asked.

"I think you two need to start doing more magic," Viola said.

"What? Why?" Casey said.

"Because I'm having issues with mine. I think it's the connection, but because you two don't use yours that often, I can't tell if there's anything wrong or if I'm having a moment."

"How long have you had the issue?" William looked more concerned than she'd seen him.

"Since we joined. I can't seem to do as much as before."

"But we can feel you trying."

"Trying is the key word." She sighed, her back falling against the desk. "I can't get a handle on what's up."

"We can try something now," Casey suggested. "See if there's anything we can't do."

"What did you used to do?"

Casey blushed. "I didn't like having to close my curtains at night. I never remembered, so I used to flick them closed."

"You've not done that this week?"

Casey frowned. "Not that I remember."

Viola pushed herself from the floor and moved to the window. She flung the curtains open, what remained of the daylight trickling through the pane.

"Try."

Casey stared at the fabric. Viola's body tingled. It was less powerful than when William had moved the cushion, but it was there. The curtains shuddered but didn't close. If she hadn't known any better, Viola would have thought there was a draught coming through the window.

"So, it's not just you."

"Not just me."

****

All three lay over the bed in some form or other while they read through the notebooks piled in Viola's room. So far, there was nothing that could be identified as the magic disappearing or weakening. William occasionally wrote something on his phone, but he didn't share any of his thoughts, no matter how many times Viola poked him in the side. Her own phone had buzzed against her side, but she didn't want to distract herself.

"We're never going to figure this out." Casey sighed.

"Shall we run away and hope no one finds us?" Viola asked, letting the notebook drop onto her face.

"As if you could leave the coven behind."

"I could try. At least I wouldn't have to deal with Ms. Glorian looking down on me all the time. I could live without that look."

"She doesn't look down on you," William murmured.

"What?"

"She doesn't look down on you. She knows what Alexander was capable of and she's worried you'll take after him. Abigail has been an Elder for a long time. I doubt there have been many who would push their magic to the limits he did, or you do." He looked at her from over the top of the notebook.

"I don't think trying to help people is something you should worry over."

"Maybe not, but it shows you have the same capability as he did. Maybe she's worried you'll try to overthrow all of them."

"Why would I want that responsibility?"

William shrugged at her as he went back to his notes.

"I give up with this hierarchy nonsense."

Casey laughed. "Who would have thought the great Viola Everett didn't have plans to take over the coven?"

She groaned. "Do people really think that?"

"There might have been one or two mentions of it in the past. At least we will be able to assuage their fears."

"Gee, thanks. I'm glad everyone thought I might make a power grab." Viola shook her head. She hadn't done anything that could have been construed as wanting anything to do with being in charge. She'd barely interacted with the coven at all.

"Think of it this way, that's the amount of power you have. And if others had it, they would be thinking of making that play. It's more a reflection of them."

"Had," Viola corrected. "I had power. Until we can figure out what's going on, no one will need to worry about me going power hungry. And also, it doesn't help to think that so many other people would be vying for control."

Casey rolled onto her side, her hand reaching out

to Viola. "We'll find a way to solve this. I trust you want to help everyone and don't only want this for some selfish reason."

"Thanks."

"Don't get used to it."

A silence settled over them for a few minutes until Viola's phone began buzzing again.

"You should probably get that," William muttered.

"It won't be important."

"How do you know if you don't check it?"

Viola sighed and pulled the device from her jeans pocket. She tried to push down the smile that rose as she read the name.

"Not that important, eh?"

"Shut up," she said as she clicked into the message chain.

"You've spent this much time with us and never once mentioned a boyfriend, or girlfriend. I thought we were friends." William held his hand over his heart, his grin plastered across his face. "When were you going to let me down?"

A laugh slipped from her. "I'm sorry to have to let you down, Will. Unfortunately, my heart is already taken."

"How did you find time to get a boyfriend with all the work and research you've been doing?" Casey asked.

"It's not a boyfriend, or girlfriend."

"Tell that to your face."

Viola refused to look at either of them. "He's not. And even if it was, it's a relationship that could never be serious."

"Rival coven?"

"More like no coven at all."

"I didn't know you were such a rebel. Look at our girl, all grown up and dating outsiders."

"Ew, you make it sound so much worse when you word it like that. If I had anything to throw at you, I would."

William laughed. "You would never want to cause me any harm."

"Don't push me."

"Is it anyone we know?"

"David Richardson."

Silence dropped around them. It was easy to forget that everyone would know who he was by name when you spent time with him. He was relaxed and normal around her.

"You know David Richardson?"

"Kind of. I mean, it was a chance meeting."

"Now I need to know everything." Casey put the notebook down and sat up.

"Fine, but it's not an interesting story."

Chapter Twenty-Three

The windows were pushed open, but smoke continued to swirl around Viola. She itched to use her energy to clean the air, but there was no guarantee it would work. She peeked into the oven. The lasagna looked perfect. No reason for all the smoke filling up the room around her.

"It's fine. It's fine," Viola repeated to herself. "I've made lasagna millions of times. I don't need to worry about this one."

She swept the fly-away hairs from in front of her face as she made up the table, placing a glass tumbler by each table mat. The places were set as knocking sounded at the kitchen door. Viola almost ran to answer it.

"Hey," she said, the words light.

David smiled at her. "Hey. I brought you this."

He offered her a bottle of wine. She didn't recognise the name on the label but didn't let the confusion show on her face. It was just a bottle of wine.

"Thanks. Do you want a glass?" she asked as she ushered him into the kitchen.

"Sure, if you don't mind."

"Nope. Let me find a more appropriate glass. Make yourself at home." Viola searched through the cabinet to find two wine glasses.

"If the food tastes as good as it smells, I think you might have won this round."

She laughed. "There was a competition? I might have upped my skills if I'd known."

She passed him the glass, taking a small sip of her own. The full-bodied flavour washed over her tongue. It was sharp, but not unpleasant. The timer on the oven chimed through the room around them. "One second." She began to pull the pans from the oven.

"Your cat is staring at me," David said above the noise of her serving the food.

"Take no notice of Ebb. She's meant to be useful, but I've not seen it from her yet. She likes to blink at people and wait for food to be handed out. Although, she's not having any of this." Viola turned to stare at the cat. She was greeted by the lazy stare she had become accustomed to.

"Is she supposed to be a guard cat or something?" he said, reaching out to stroke the tabby.

"If she is, I need a refund."

Ebb chirped under David's hand. She pushed his hand up as she tried to move closer to him.

"Why is your cat broken?" he asked.

"She's not broken. She speaks a foreign language."

"All the better to lull the birds from the branches."

"I don't think I've ever seen her catch a bird before," Viola said as she crossed the short space to place the lasagna in the middle of the table. "I don't think I've ever seen her react to a stranger like that either. She must like you."

"How does she normally react?"

"Scratching, hissing, and that's if she's in a good mood." Viola shrugged. "Maybe I need to take her to a vet."

"That's cruel. She clearly has the ability to see pure and trustworthy souls." He winked at her.

Viola rolled her eyes. "Tuck in. There should be more than enough here."

"It does look more like you're trying to feed a stadium rather than two people."

"I like leftovers." She smiled, her plate already adorned with food.

"I'll try to leave you some."

"There best be more than some," she said playfully as she scooped a piece of lasagna onto her fork.

They ate in almost silence. When either of them tried to speak to the other, they were greeted with a mouth full of food and an apologetic smile.

"This tastes amazing. It's like restaurant quality," David said between bites.

"I'm taking that as a win."

"I would happily lose if it meant you made more food like this."

"Only if you're making more pasta from scratch."

"Deal." He grinned at her.

****

"Viola, I'm home early," Emilia called as Viola heard the door close. "Have you eaten yet?"

Viola's face dropped as she whispered, "I'm sorry, David. I thought I'd remembered to let her know about tonight."

"You don't have to be sorry. You don't have to hide me from everyone."

"I'm sure you don't want me announcing your location online."

David grimaced. "No, I don't want that, but you've met my parents. Meeting parent charm, or meeting a fan charm?"

"What?"

Viola didn't have time to process his request as her mum pushed open the door.

"Oh, Vi. I didn't realise you had a guest," Emilia said. She looked at David. Lines etched on her brow. "Do I know you?"

He flashed her a smile. "Maybe not in person." He stood from his chair and held out his hand. "David Richardson."

"David Richardson?" Emilia said, taking a small step backwards.

Viola noticed the moment recognition flashed through her mum's eyes. It was brief, but it was there. As the look passed, Emilia's face softened into a smile.

"Oh, you must be who's distracted Viola so much recently." Emilia pressed her hand into his. "I will get out of your way and leave you two to it." She moved her attention to Viola. "Let me know when you're done, and I'll head back." She half-turned back to David before leaving the room. "It was a pleasure to meet you. I'm sorry to intrude."

Viola sat, waiting for the sound of the front door to close before she spoke.

"You never told your mum about me?" David beat her to it.

"I said I wouldn't tell anyone," she said. "I didn't think I'd need to mention anything to her. But then we bumped into each other again…" Viola trailed off.

"Thank you," David said, his words barely audible.

"You're welcome."

****

Their plates lay empty on the table. Viola's worry and nerves from the morning had slowly dissipated. All her nerves had been for nothing. She should have known it would go smoothly.

"Is it just you and your mum here?" David asked, breaking her from her thoughts.

"Yep, and Ebb. Don't forget about her," she answered. "Being a nurse might seem glamourous, but it doesn't pay enough to live alone. At least not as newly qualified as I am. Not that I mind still being at home. It's always been Mum and me."

"What about your dad? Do you see him often?"

Viola dropped her gaze. "He died when I was young."

"I'm sorry." David reached across the table towards her.

"You don't have to be," she said as she pushed the sadness down. "It was so long ago, and it's not like you knew."

"Still, I'm sorry. I'm sure he'd be proud of you."

"That's what everyone tells me, but I wish it could

be him telling me instead of other people. Maybe he would hate the music I listen to, or he'd want me to have travelled more." The corners of her mouth lifted. "It's difficult hearing what people think he would have thought."

"How long ago was it? If you don't mind me asking."

"About twenty years or so. The worst part is I don't remember much about him now. I didn't have enough time to memorise everything I could."

"You don't have to feel bad about that. You can't remember everything, and you were what? Five? Don't feel like you're failing if you forget things."

"I'm worried that one day, I won't have any memories left. The ones I have are worn with my mind going over them as often as I do." Viola hadn't admitted this to anyone else before. She hadn't had anyone who she felt safe enough with to say it. She felt lighter from saying it, but she was worried how David would react to it.

He had inched closer to her as she spoke without her noticing. As she realised. his presence engulfed her. Her energy hummed at his proximity.

His hand ghosted across the top of hers. "Has anyone told you that you worry too much? Your memories might get a little fuzzy as you get older, but you'll always have them. Do you have any pictures of him?"

Viola nodded before she answered. "There are a few in frames around the house."

"Then you'll never forget him. There will be something for you to concentrate your memories on to keep his face present. I can't say that you won't forget.

I've never had to deal with anything like this. But I don't think you should make yourself feel bad for something out of your control."

"Thanks," she said. "Sometimes I feel like I should be doing more to remember him."

"Don't add another worry into your already filled mind." He smiled, the corners crinkling. "There isn't a test for you to pass on how much you can remember him."

"Are you sure?" Her own smile joined his.

Their easy conversation flowed until David excused himself for the night. Viola leaned her back against the door after she had locked him out. Would her dad be proud of the decisions she had been making with his work? She tried not to let her thoughts bring down her mood from the evening.

Chapter Twenty-Four

"Why isn't this working?" Viola said, kicking the bottom of the wall.

"Staying calm might help," William said.

"We don't have time to be messing around with this. We've already failed at the protection once, and now we can't do anything."

"No, we don't have time. And you throwing a temper tantrum isn't going to help. I'd have thought being a nurse would have taught you some patience," Casey said, staring at her.

"Why do I need patience when I can help speed things along?"

"You don't." Casey's eyes went wide.

"Not all the time, but sometimes a little push helps more than if we let things go naturally. It's no different than using medication to break a fever."

"And you wondered why someone was watching

the hospital? Your impatience could have exposed this entire coven. Has no one ever noticed you don't have to wait as long for your patients to heal?"

"It's never come up."

"You're so arrogant." Casey pinched the bridge of her nose and took a deep breath before she continued. "I can't believe I joined my magic up with you." There was anger in her words, but also a hint of betrayal. As though Viola had managed to break a piece of trust that she didn't know Casey had placed in her.

"It's not arrogant." Viola started to feel a little awkward under Casey's intense gaze.

"Then what is it?"

"Not being able to stand by and do nothing. We have this chance to help people, but we hide away. I refuse to be like that. We should be helping."

"So, you'd risk us all for your own self-righteousness?"

"How is it self-righteous?"

"Because you think feeling better about yourself is better than keeping the coven safe. You don't get to choose to put us all in danger."

"Viola, Casey. Come on. Don't let this get to you. We need to work together, not argue over something petty," William said.

Viola pressed her fingers to her forehead. "I'm not arguing, but I'm not wrong. We've all cowered and hidden when we could have been doing something worthwhile." She grabbed her bag from the table. "I'll talk to you later. I can't be here."

"Good riddance," Casey called after her.

****

"Viola, wait up."

Viola continued her forward march. Arrogant, that was what they thought of her. She thought they had gotten past this. She racked her brain, but there was nothing she could think of that would push anyone to think of her in that light. If this was how Casey thought of her after everything they'd talked about, she might as well go it alone. If William hadn't spoken to her, none of this would have happened. She might have found a workable way by now.

Footsteps pounded behind her. "You really are on a mission, huh?" William said, his voice a little out of breath.

"Go away."

"No. Storming off isn't going to help anyone."

She brushed his arm off her shoulder. "William, I'm not in the mood."

"Running away won't help anyone."

"I'm not running away. I'm removing myself from the situation. There's a difference."

"Okay, but we need to do this as a team."

"Or I can find a way to break us apart and I'll go back to doing what I do best."

"Isolating yourself isn't the answer to your, no, our problems."

"I've done pretty all right for the past twenty years. Twenty years where no one cared enough to help me out or do anything to help. And yet, because I can't sit back and do nothing, I should feel bad about it. No, I was right all along. It's easier to do things on your own. You don't have to worry about what anyone else thinks or how they think you should do something."

Viola thrust her hands into her jacket pockets. Her

pace quickened as she tried to put distance between her and William.

His now-familiar footsteps faded from her ears, but she refused to slow her own. She needed space away from both of them before she did something she'd regret. Maybe if there was some space between them, she would be able to use her magic without either of them knowing what she was doing. A few weeks ago, she'd been so happy to be able to join their magic together. It was proof they were making the right steps. But now, it was a reminder that they hadn't been able to work out anything further.

****

She pulled the coat tighter across her body. The evening chill forced its way through the seams and gaps to run against her skin. She shivered. Why was she so annoyed by their disagreement? From the moment they'd worked together, it was clear Casey didn't have a high opinion of her. It shouldn't have made any difference that they were still falling out. But it did.

Viola hoped that the time they'd spent together would help to dissuade some of the long-held beliefs. If she couldn't show Casey that she only wanted the best for everyone, was there any point in continuing with the work they were doing?

She kicked at the loose stones on the path. The action stopped her thoughts from spiralling, but it didn't give her any ideas on how to stop their fighting.

"If Casey wasn't so stubborn, this would be much easier," she muttered to herself, the irony of her own thinking not lost on her. Changing her thoughts would be much harder than wishing her somewhat friend would see where she was coming from.

She meandered down the path, veering into the nearside field. She should have gone home, but in a way, that would have been admitting defeat. She found herself moving towards a bench not too far from the path. She sat and pulled her legs as close to her chest as she could. Just once, she'd like to be able to talk to someone about how she felt. To let out all her frustration and have someone understand where she was coming from. She hadn't been able to find a therapist who would understand any of her rants on the magic community.

It didn't take long from the chill to move from the metal seating into her legs. Viola slowly unfurled from the bench and braced herself for the questions her mum was sure to ask her. She didn't want to have to see the concern on her mum's face anymore.

She moved in the general direction of her house. The closer she edged towards the road, the more she felt her resistance. A few more minutes in the cold couldn't be too painful, could it? Lost in her internal struggles, she didn't notice the car pulling up alongside her.

"Penny for your thoughts?" David asked her from the window.

Startled, she instinctively took a step back. "What?"

"You looked lost. Do you need me to take you home?"

"No, I'm fine."

"You don't look fine."

"I will be, no need to worry." Her eyebrows dipped. "What are you doing around here?"

She swore his eyes flicked towards her house. "I was in the neighbourhood. But while I'm here, do you want to get in? I can promise to smooth out those worry lines."

"I've not got any other plans for the evening."

"You know how to make a guy feel wanted."

David opened his door before moving across to allow her room to get in.

Chapter Twenty-Five

"This might be the nicest hot chocolate I've had." Viola sighed as she took a sip from the mug in her hand.

"The secret ingredient is real chocolate," David said.

Viola choked on her drink. "I thought you were going to say crime." She took another sip. "It should be criminal with how good this is."

"I'm glad my talents with milk and chocolate have come into good use."

"You and me both, David."

Viola sighed and relaxed further into the sofa.

"You going to tell me why you were out wandering around in the cold on your own?"

"It's embarrassing."

"It can't be that bad."

She sighed and closed her eyes. "I had a fight with my friends, and I might have stormed off."

"That bad of a fight?"

"It wasn't anything important. Well, I mean, they insulted me. But I don't know if they're right." Viola paused. "Do you think I'm arrogant?"

David's eyebrows shot up. "Arrogant? You? It's not the first word I'd think of when I think of you. I don't think it would reach my top hundred."

"You might not have spent enough time with me." She smiled weakly. "I don't think I'm cocky, but some of the things they said were right. I don't always think of how my actions could harm other people I—"

"That doesn't make you arrogant." David cut her off. "Lacking in foresight, but not arrogant."

David placed his cup on the coffee table as he moved closer to her. He reached out and pushed a stray strand of hair from her face. Heat rose to her cheeks. She hoped the familiar red stain had not followed the feeling.

"I'm sure the fight won't have caused too much friction between you. You'll be friends again in no time."

"You weren't there. Things were said that I don't think any of us will be able to get over."

David cupped her cheek and looked into her eyes. The stare made her want to run away from what was happening, but before she could he started to speak.

"There are only a few things that cause irreparable damage. You might have bruised egos, but I believe that you will be able to resolve it."

"I don't know, it was pretty heated," Viola murmured, attempting to stop her body from falling into his touch.

"If you're friends, it won't be a problem. And if

they aren't able to get over it, maybe you weren't really friends."

Viola scrunched up her face as she placed her cup next to his. "That's what I'm worried about. How can you tell if someone is your friend?"

"If you're having to ask, then maybe they aren't."

"We kind of grew up together, but we never spoke until recently. I think I'm worried the reason they stayed away all these years was because everyone was right about me."

David stared at her. "Everyone? You didn't get a break from anyone at school?"

She chose not to correct him his assumption. "It wasn't only people my own age." An easier admission to make.

He stared at her. "Not just…" he trailed off. "The parents were in on it to. The actual adults." He ran his hand over his face as he continued to stare at her.

Viola nodded.

"Fully grown adults were badmouthing a child to other children, and you think you're the issue. You really need to get better friends, and maybe better acquaintances."

He pulled her into him. His warmth lulled her. She settled against his chest. "Thanks," she murmured. "Sometimes it's hard to remember that." Her arms snaked around his middle, pulling him closer to her.

"I want you to know how important you are. Don't let other people get in your head."

"Thanks, but I think I was to blame for some of it. Or at least for some of my outburst. I don't know if I've messed up too much, though." She sighed as she extricated herself from him. "Thank you for the hot chocolate, but I should head home and see how much damage control needs to be done."

"Any time, Vi. Don't feel like you can only come and see me when you're having a crisis."

****

Viola snuck into the house, not wanting to wake her mum up at the late hour, but she needn't have worried as the living room light was still on.

"Mum?" Viola called.

"Oh, love, I didn't realise what time it was," Emilia said as she walked into the hallway. "Where have you been?"

"With David, but what about you? What have you been doing?" Viola asked.

Emilia looked back into the room. "I thought I could try and do something to help. It's not a lot, but I wanted to see if I could understand anything your dad had written."

Viola moved forward to give her a hug. "Thank you."

"You're welcome. Plus, I know you're having a hard time. There's barely been any of your energy around the house for a few days." Emilia held up her hand. "No, you don't have to tell me about it if you don't want to share. But I thought the stress of everything might be getting to you."

Viola felt tears well up. "It's been a lot," she managed to get to out.

"It has for everyone, but you don't have to keep all your emotions locked up in there." She playfully tapped Viola's head.

Viola's tears fell freely. "Mum, I think I've messed up again."

"What do you mean? What's happened?"

"What always happens. I put my guard up and lashed out. Casey has never liked me, and everything the coven has ever said about me is right. I do flout the rules and do what I want. I never listen to what anyone says, and I always think I know best. I thought we were getting past it, but then we tried something, and it didn't work. We both said words we might regret. How am I supposed to get her to want to work with me when deep down she doesn't believe I want to help the coven?"

"Have you apologised?"

"No, but it—"

"Then you know what need to do," Emilia said as she stared at her daughter.

"But what if she doesn't accept it?"

"Then you'll have to find a way for her to accept it. I know you've never been close, but in the past few months, you've been on good terms. That will count for something. You both need to swallow your pride and figure out a way to resolve these differences once and for all."

Viola rubbed the tears from her face. "Why do you always use reason on me?"

"Because sometimes you don't use it on yourself." Emilia smiled as she let go of her. "Do you want me to show you what I found?"

"Of course."

With the tension dropping from her body, she followed her mum into the living room. As she crossed the threshold, she was startled. Her mum had arranged the notebooks around the room, and in the centre, she had created a circle.

"Your dad was obsessed with loops in his drawing, so I created one to see what he was doing."

"I don't think we need a salt circle in the middle of the living room."

"Very funny. But it got me thinking, what if that was his aim?"

Viola stopped. Wasn't that the very thing they had been coming up with? She felt her heart beat faster; they must be on the right track if her mum had seen it too.

"Mum, do you know if there's anywhere in the coven that links us all together?"

Emilia frowned. "I don't think I know what you mean."

Deflated, Viola waved her hand. "Never mind. It was just a theory we had."

"For what?"

"Okay, so the protection would need to be anchored somewhere to keep the coven safe, but where would that be?"

"And it would have to work for High Peak as well," her mum mumbled. "No, there's nothing I can think of that would have us all linked in that way."

"That's what we've been thinking. No one has confirmed anything. But the protection had to have been placed somewhere."

"You'll figure it out."

"Thanks." Viola looked at everything in the room. "Do you need any help with this, or am I all right to head to bed?"

"You go. I've got this." Emilia turned to tidy up the

books. "If I think of anything else, I'll let you know."

Viola headed to bed. She was resolved to fix things between her and Casey and get their magic working as soon as she was rested.

Chapter Twenty-Six

Viola left the hospital and waited until she had crossed the road before picking up her phone. She'd left a hasty message in the group chat that morning but hadn't had the chance to check it since then. She had been left on read. One deep breath later, she sent another message. They needed to make sure that they were all on the same page.

She pulled the phone to her ear. "Will, we need to meet. All of us, but Casey seems to be against me again."

"Well, you have had a habit of bailing when things get tough." His exasperation was evident through the phone.

"I know. But that was more so I could sort myself out. I wasn't ditching."

"It didn't look that way."

"I know. Please can you help her meet me so we can sort this out once and for all?"

"I will, but don't think you can keep doing this."

"You're the best. I promise I'm changing my ways."

"We hope so." His words belied the smile she could hear.

"Let me know where you want to meet, and I'll be there."

"Will do, bye."

The phone disconnected. Viola waited for his message as she climbed onto the bus. She had a feeling it would either be at her house or Casey's. At least she would still be going in the same direction. She practised in her head what she wanted to say. She needed Casey... well, both of them, to know that she found it difficult to rely on others, and this was all new ground for her. She thought she'd been able to explain that before, but maybe she hadn't been as clear as she hoped.

As she alighted the bus, she got a message.

Meet at yours. W

Perfect. She didn't know how long they would take to get there, but at least she would be in the comfort of her own home.

She unlocked the door and went into the living room. Ebb found her way to her side. Viola lowered her hand and scratched at her pet's head.

"Hey, lovely. Have you had a good day?" The cat purred under her hand. "I'll get you some food in a second."

She checked to make sure the house was still protected. There wasn't anything she could do if it wasn't, but she needed to put her own mind at ease as she waited. When the knock came at the door, she almost launched herself at it with the adrenaline coursing through her.

"Casey, William." She gestured for them to enter.

"You know, I've never been here unless there's been a meeting," Casey said as Viola showed them into the living room.

"There would have been no reason for you to have before." Viola shrugged.

"Ladies, please." William sat down in the middle of the sofa.

"What do you need to say to me?" Casey asked, ignoring William's look.

"It's to both of you." Viola gathered her thoughts. "I can't do this alone. But that's not the only reason I need you two. I've never had to rely on anyone else. I've never had anyone else want to be there for me and I didn't realise how much I was missing from my life. I'm not the best at showing it, but I mean it. I'm sorry for how I stormed off the other day. It wasn't me throwing a tantrum. I was overwhelmed and needed somewhere to regulate myself again. I know it's not an excuse." She held up her hand to wave off their attempts to interrupt. "But it is the truth. I need you both, and I'm willing to do what it takes for you to believe me."

She waited for them to say something.

"That was very open of you," William said cautiously. "I don't need you to apologise but to let us in."

"I'm trying."

"Casey?" he prompted.

Casey's shoulders slumped. "It can't have been easy for you all this time. But if you can show us that you mean it, then we can work through it. That doesn't mean you're completely forgiven, though."

"I wouldn't have thought it would." Viola smiled at them.

"You might regret saying you would do anything, though."

"Maybe, but whatever it takes. Now, there's something I should tell you."

Viola's sentence was interrupted as all of their phones vibrated, and her energy rippled through her.

"What is with all these meetings?" Casey huffed after quickly scanning through the message and putting the phone back into her pocket.

"I guess we're in a heightened security phase," Viola said.

"Let's hope it's not bad news this time." William stood and walked to the door.

****

They squeezed their way into Ms. Glorian's house. The few people Viola noticed had the same confused expression. It seemed no one knew what this meeting was for.

"Everyone, settle down," Ms. Glorian requested to the assembled crowd. "I'm thankful you could all make your way here with such short notice. And I'm aware that the number of meetings we've been holding has been abnormally large of late. However, we are in a precarious situation." She moved to the stand where everyone could see her. "There have been no new developments with either of the missing women, but we are doing everything we can to locate them. We've had no demands from the witch hunter. We're unsure if this is a positive sign or not, but their families are being looked after in the eventuality of a more upsetting outcome."

"Is this all we've been brought here for?" Viola asked, the words slipping from her. Her hands clenched at her sides.

Ms. Glorian regarded her coolly. "This meeting is to discuss whether the current security measures have been working."

Viola felt her cheeks flush but bit back the words she wanted to unleash. Their current predicament was not something that would help them. They all knew it, but no one else would dare to question the Elders.

"As I was saying," Ms. Glorian continued. "We are doing what we can for the families and in our efforts to find the young women, but we have noted that the current security measures have been helping to keep everyone under the radar. The Elders have been meeting to decide if this should be enacted countrywide or remain localised to our two covens. For the time being, we will continue as we are, and everyone is to report any suspicious behaviour to me..."

Viola tuned out the rest of the speech. She needed to figure out how to get the protection back in place before the Elders could force everyone into hiding. What would hiding do to keep them safe? It would only make the other covens weaker, and if anything happened, they wouldn't be able to resolve it. No, she wouldn't let this happen to everyone. She looked at Casey and could see from the determined set of her face that she wouldn't let that happen either. The other woman caught her eye and gave a curt nod. Viola was surprised at the agreement.

"We will be reconvening every fortnight until we are sure the danger has passed." Ms. Glorian finished her speech. "Please continue to follow the rules and keep a watch for anything that seems untoward."

Viola held back the snort as much as she could. As if they would do anything if they did report it. No one had listened to her or taken her concerns seriously. She turned to her two friends. "Shall we continue?"

They nodded at her as they went to leave the house. As she stepped through the threshold, she caught sight of Thomas. If she could speak to him now, they might be able to get through this quicker than anticipated. She turned around to make her way to him but lost sight of where he'd gone. She twisted around her, but it was as if he had vanished.

William pulled at her arm. "What are you doing?"

"I thought I would be able to get a hold of Thomas before he left." She looked down the darkened path. "Did you see which way he went?"

Chapter Twenty-Seven

William's eyebrows scrunched together. "Why would you need to know where he'd gone?"

"He's my next lead."

"Lead on what?" Casey interrupted.

"Getting our magic to work. There was something I was told a few weeks ago, but I didn't have a reason to follow it up before."

Viola let the silence hang between them all.

"I guess that makes sense," William said.

"Why would he know something?" Casey asked.

"I think he might have been one of my dad's friends. If my mum doesn't know the answers, then maybe he confided in someone else."

"It can't hurt to ask him," William agreed.

"You can let me know if he was any use when you're making it up to me," Casey said.

Viola sighed. "You're really not going to let that

go?"

"Nope."

"Fine. Text me when you're free and I'll do what you want."

Casey's eyes sparkled. "You might regret that."

"Whatever. Do you know where Thomas lives?"

"Yeah."

Casey gave her the address and left Viola to make her own way there. Now she had a concrete lead, the nerves settled in. Her fingers tapped along her palms as she waited for her bus to reach its stop. It should only be a short walk, and she hoped Thomas would be willing to see her. If he'd been one of her dad's best friends, why had he never spoken to her about him?

What if I've got this all wrong?

She closed her eyes and exhaled slowly through her mouth. The bus jerked to a stop, and Viola left with a quick thanks thrown over her shoulder to the driver. She looked at her phone to check which road to take and set off.

As the house came into view, she clenched her hands into fists. If she showed for a moment that she was worried, she wouldn't be able to get herself to do what she needed to. She rapped her knuckles against the door and took a small step back.

"Hello?" Thomas queried as he opened the door on her.

"Hi, I'm sorry to bother you, but I'm—"

"Viola," he finished for her. "I know who you are."

Her cheeks reddened. "Yeah, of course. I hoped I could ask you a couple of questions about my dad."

"Your mum know you're here?"

"No."

"Look, I'd like to help, but I know how Emilia feels about me. I don't want to deal with her if you get yourself caught up in something you shouldn't."

"Please. I don't care how my mum feels about this, she knows that once I've decided on something there's no stopping me. I think you can help." She paused. "It's about the magic he was working on."

"Give me strength," he muttered under his hand as it wiped down his face, tugging on his beard. "Come inside. We shouldn't be talking about this on the street."

****

The living room was small and dark. The walls were painted a dark grey with the furniture falling into the same colour palette. The lack of colour or personality felt jarring to Viola.

"What have you been doing that means you need to come to me?" Thomas asked her. His dark eyes pierced into her light ones.

"I've been going through my dad's notebooks, but I think I need someone who knew what he was doing to help me."

"And you've been pointed in my direction?" The look he gave her wasn't one to inspire confidence in this being a fruitful meeting.

"I was told someone outspoken used to spend a lot of time with my dad. You were the most outspoken at the meeting today, so it made sense."

"Alex said it would be anger that would get me into trouble." Thomas sighed as he sank into one of the chairs. He gestured for Viola to do the same.

"Can you help me?" She leaned forward in her seat

"I would love to, but he didn't speak to anyone about what he was doing. I can't help."

Viola narrowed her eyes. "If that was true, why were you worried if my mum knew where I was? Has she told you not to speak to me?"

"What? No! She held a lot of resentment for what happened. She thought I could have helped him. It's easier to blame someone living than someone you loved who succeeded with their suicide mission."

"You do know what he did, then?"

Thomas blanched. "Shit. Look, Viola, me and your dad were good at what we did. We were close friends, but he decided that his life wasn't worth keeping safe. Even when he had you and your mum, he put himself in harm's way to save other people. I'm not telling you anything that will set you off down the same path. I won't sit back and watch Emilia suffer through the same thing twice. Do yourself a favour and stay away."

"It might be too late for that."

"What did you do?"

"We tried to put more protection in place, but it didn't work. Then we figured out that Dad knew how to link people together." She had the grace to drop her gaze.

"At least Emilia can't blame me for that." Thomas sighed. "Is that what you need help with?"

"Yes… no. Sort of," she answered. "We might have lost the ability to practice or interact with our power. Or at least do anything too intensive."

"Idiot. I told him to stop with the riddles." He covered his eyes with his hand. "I need you to tell me what you did, and I'll see if I can get you unstuck."

"We don't want to be unstuck. We want access back

to the energy we have."

"Fine, I'll tell you how to manage that. But don't get yourself killed with this. It's not fair on your mum."

Viola's head dropped. "I know, but I can't let everyone else die." Her voice came out small.

"I know, kid."

****

Viola held her phone to her ear as she ran towards the bus stop.

"Pick up, pick up, pick up," she muttered to the dialling tone.

"Viola?" The voice was hesitant.

"Casey, try some magic."

"What?"

"Thomas showed me how to fix it. You should be able to use yours now."

There was a slight pause and then a small squeak through the phone. "It worked."

Viola grinned. "Perfect. We had tightened the connection too much. Don't ask me how it works as I didn't understand what he was saying, but it was almost like the connections we'd made were suffocating our own abilities."

"And you were able to loosen it?"

"Thomas walked me through it. Because we're linked, I could do it for all of us."

"Thanks for letting me know."

"You're welcome. I'm trying that 'not being isolated thing' you keep saying I do."

"It had to stay with you at some point."

Viola could almost hear the smile through the

phone.

Chapter Twenty-Eight

"When you said I had more to do to make it up to you, I didn't expect torture."

"Tsk. Torture is going a bit far, isn't it?" Casey responded, flick her hair over her shoulder.

Viola grimaced as Casey applied the final nail to her hand. "You know I can't keep this on. We have to keep our nails short and unvarnished in the hospital."

"I know, but I need the practice. It will give me a chance to soak them off as well. You won't have to worry about them for too long."

The blue nails glittered at her. Viola sighed. "I don't have a shift for a few days. It would be a waste to get rid of them straight away when you've gone to so much effort."

"You must really be trying to get my forgiveness."

"No, I'm trying to stop being so pig-headed all the time. I thought you'd approve."

Casey didn't respond, but Viola could see a small smile forming on the other woman's face.

"It would be a shame to lose such a great piece of work so quickly. When do you need them gone by?"

"Friday."

"I'm free Thursday night. Come over and I'll sort it out for you."

They sat in silence as Casey finished Viola's nails. The shade matched the colour of the dress Viola had thrown on before leaving the house. She wished she could find a way to keep them, but short of leaving her job, she knew it wouldn't be achievable.

"Am I forgiven?" Viola asked.

"Not in the slightest," Casey said as she held back a snort. "But I haven't given up hope on you. You're not as bad as everyone says."

"I knew I'd be able to win you over."

"I wouldn't say won over, but maybe more worn down."

"As long as you get to see the real me, I don't mind so much." Viola admired the nails again. "Did you do this without any magic? I know I didn't feel any, but they are amazing."

Casey beamed. "No, this is something I wanted to be able to do by myself. To take pride in something that I could do without any help."

"So, that's why you were so mad at me."

Casey's hand stilled. "I guess. Knowing that you used your magic to do your work annoyed me. Why wouldn't you want to be able to do it without?"

"Because if I use it, then I can make sure more people live. I don't want to let anyone down if I don't have to."

"Wouldn't you feel better knowing you'd done it on your own, though? That you hadn't had a helping hand from something else?"

"I am doing it on my own. Being a witch is who I am and I'm not ashamed of that. I get that we've been hidden away for so long, but I don't think we should push it aside. If that means I annoy people with what I'm using, then so be it."

Casey looked at her. Viola squirmed under the scrutiny. "I've never thought of it that way before." She admitted.

"I wish more people would. Maybe they would stop whispering about me whenever I enter a room."

"They don't do that."

Viola looked at Casey. The disbelief was written over her face as Casey turned away. "You don't have to lie to make me feel better."

"Okay. They don't do it all the time."

Viola opened her mouth to respond when she heard her phone. She picked it up from the table and saw a message from her mum.

"Oh, that's strange. Another meeting's been called. It's not been two weeks yet though, has it?"

Casey shook her head. "It's got to be something important for Abigail to change the schedule she put in place. Come on. We'd better get there to see how important it is," Casey said as she pushed herself from the chair.

****

"I'm sorry to have called you all here with such short notice again," Ms. Glorian said, her voice carrying to each of them. "We have received the worst news today. The missing girl, Sophie, from High Peak, has been found." She quietened the murmurs erupting around her. Viola placed her hand on William's arm as he stiffened beside her. "Her body was located a few hours ago, not too far from her home. The Elder from High Peak has suggested that it was deliberately staged for us to find."

Her words settled on them, their importance not lost on the coven. They weren't safe. Even if the protection spell had worked, it would have been too late. The hunter already knew where they were and how to find them.

Viola's thoughts swirled, dizzying as they crashed down on her. There wasn't any way to keep them safe. Had the past few months gone to waste? She struggled to concentrate on the rest of Ms. Glorian's speech. It was pointless. Her dad's sacrifice had meant nothing. He could have been here with her. *No.* She couldn't think like that. If he hadn't done what he had, they could have been found sooner, and there was no guarantee he wouldn't have been found.

"Unfortunately, we still have no word on Evie. We must presume she is still in the clutches of the hunter. We're unsure if this is the same one who has targeted High Peak. On the back of this, we have spoken about not allowing members to go out on their own. However, the logistics of this would be unmanageable with people going to different places of work."

"How are we going to keep safe?" someone shouted.

"We are doing everything we can to ensure we won't be detected—"

"You've been saying that for months. Alex's protection is almost gone and we're already seeing the results of it. Something needs to be done."

"They're right!" someone else shouted. "None of us are safe."

"Everyone, stay calm. We have this under control, and we are reviewing our contingency plans," Ms. Glorian said, her voice resounding around the room.

Viola scoffed. The Elders had no idea what they needed to do, and they were too proud to ask.

William nudged her arm. "You might want to change the look on your face," he whispered.

She quickly softened her expression. "Thanks."

"They're annoying me too, but we don't want to upset them before we can do anything to help."

"I don't understand why the coven doesn't want us to do anything. Isn't this serious enough for them to consider what my dad did before? Someone is dead. Someone they could have helped save." She pulled at the hem of her sleeve. "I don't know why Thomas didn't want to help."

"He might not have known everything, but at least he did what he could."

"I suppose."

"Look, we don't need to be so down about this. We can still fix it, even without the Elders agreeing. Once we've figured out why it didn't work last time, the Elders will quake at our abilities."

"Are you sure we don't need anyone else?" Viola worried at her lip, ignoring his attempts to lighten the mood.

"I can't believe you're suggesting extra help."

"You've rubbed off on me. Maybe in the worst

way."

William paused, his expression turning serious. "Have you found anything else in your dad's notebooks? No hints at how many people might be needed to get this to work? No, three is the correct number and the perfect amount? Going up to five would mean we've gone too far."

She shook her head. "Not in so many words. But I can't help but think that it didn't work because we're not strong enough."

"We'd have to find a way to convince more people in the coven. You know they will be wary of doing what we have."

She turned her attention back to the meeting, but the words washed over her. Her phone buzzed in her pocket, distracting her even more than before. She slipped the device into her hand. David's name flashed on the screen and a smile spread across her face, eating away at the worry that had been there moments before.

"Lover boy?" William whispered.

"He is not."

"But you want him to be. No one smiles like that for a friend."

"Fine, we've been seeing each other. But we've not had much time to ourselves. I don't have time for a real relationship. Not when we have to deal with all this."

"Doesn't he understand?"

"He's not a witch. I can't tell him what's happening."

"Oh." William paused. "Not a great time to try and initiate a non-witch into the coven."

"I've tried to hide as much as possible, but I don't know if this is going to be something serious. I don't know if it's worth causing issues for a short fling."

"It must be difficult for the great Viola Everett to hide her magic away." The grin almost covered his entire face.

Viola elbowed him in the ribs. "At least I've practised my magic for the past twenty years. Imagine how much more serious this would be if I hadn't."

"What are you two conspiring about?" Casey asked as she made her way over to their corner.

"Viola's love interest and his lack of magical abilities and awareness."

Casey rolled her eyes. "Really? You think now is a good time for a relationship?"

"No." Viola huffed. "You know it's nothing serious. It's been a couple of dates over the past few months. I didn't think it would get as serious as it is now. I didn't even think he would be staying in the city."

"You're still seeing David?"

"Yeah."

"Oh, wow. I didn't expect that to be such a long-term thing. Not that I'm saying anything against you, but I thought he wouldn't be in one place too long."

"This is why he's still in the dark. I thought he would be a nice escape while he was around, but he's still here."

"Ooh, Casey, we might have started to get her to open up. Did we only need to investigate her love life? We could have done this weeks ago."

Casey smiled at Viola's discomfort. "I'm glad I know about this now. There's still time to put this to good use."

"Gee, thanks. I'm glad my relationship dilemmas are a source of interest for you."

The crowd moved around them, some people heading for the doors while others moved towards the front.

"I think we missed the meeting," William said.

"I think we got the most important message," Casey said. "They're still too scared to do anything."

"You've got that right…" Viola started as she saw Emilia make her way towards them.

"Casey, William." Emilia acknowledged her friends before she turned to Viola. "Viola, come. We need to go home and prepare."

"Prepare for what?" She looked at her friends, but their blank expressions didn't help.

Emilia blinked at them. "I guess all three of you may need to come back to the house. I'll fill you in when we get there."

Emilia walked away, leaving Casey, Viola, and William to follow, confused.

****

"You three need to pay more attention in these meetings," Emilia warned as she handed them drinks. "I know what you've been up to, and you more than any others in that room need to know what's happening."

"What did we miss that was important? Everyone was talking over the top of each other," Viola said.

"Abigail added in more restrictions."

"Seriously? What else can we be restricted on?"

"No meeting with people outside the coven, except for work."

"Looks like you have an even more doomed

relationship." William laughed.

Viola glared at him. "If you weren't holding that tea, I would throw a cushion at you."

"This is serious. The coven is on a strict lockdown. If you don't know what you need to do to perform the spell, you need to work it out fast. Otherwise, you might have to give it up."

"We might not be able to completely give it up," Viola admitted.

Emilia's eyes narrowed. "What do you mean?"

"We may have figured out how to link our magic together so we can share the energy between us," Casey said.

Emilia slowly sat back into the chair. Her eyes closed as she massaged her temples. "How did I not see this coming? Why did Alex have to make that bit clear? Is this what you were annoying Thomas over?"

"You understood that bit in his notes?" Viola asked, purposely ignoring her mum's final question.

"Of course I did. He was my husband. There were some things he wasn't able to keep completely locked up with his ridiculous riddles. But I didn't want you to run off and do the same as him, or at least what I suspected he did. If only the rest of it made more sense."

"At least it wasn't only us struggling to understand it," William said.

"No, it wasn't." Emilia sighed. "What I wouldn't give for him to have told me his plan. But if I'd known, I'd have tried to stop him. I should be stopping you three from doing the same thing."

"Do you know anyone else he might have linked his magic with?"

"If you couldn't get anything out of Thomas, then there's no one else I know you can ask. I don't know if he ever managed to achieve it, or if it was only theories. I hope for your sake he didn't. If he performed the final spell on his own, it might have been what caused his downfall, but it could keep you three safe."

"Do you think three people is enough to get the protection in place and stop the hunter from finding more of us?" Viola asked.

"No, I don't. Do you have any of his notebooks to hand and any of your notes? I can have a look to see if anything else makes sense. It's how I worked out the linking magic." She shook her head. "I can't believe you did this."

"We had to do something, Mum."

"I know, but I wish you didn't have to be so like your dad." Emilia smiled weakly. "But I am glad this coven has some witches who want to help instead of running scared."

"Mrs. Everett," William said.

"Call me Emilia, please."

"Emilia," he said, the word sounding unsure from his mouth. "You said we need to pay more attention. It can't have only been this extra rule we missed."

"No, it wasn't. The Elders have arranged for dampeners to be placed around our houses to stop the use of magic from being detected." She held up her hands. "It sounds like a great thing, but this will also cause the use of our magic to be weakened. With the rules limiting where we can practice, I'm unsure if this was not a deliberate choice. It may, however, cause you a few issues with the final pieces of your research."

"How long until every house is covered?"

"I'd say about a week."

"That's what they think," Viola said. "I bet I can find a way to limit detection without it causing an issue with how much we can use." Her voice came out lower than she anticipated.

Silence settled around them, no one wanting to comment on the subtle threat laced within Viola's words. They would have to hope a week would be long enough to unearth the final pieces, or at the very least, long enough for counter magic to be put in place.

"Viola, Will," Casey said. "If it's easier, or if it speeds things up, you can stay with me for the next week. We can practise when we've finished work, as long as we don't kill each other before."

"Are you sure?" Viola asked.

Casey nodded. "The coven needs every bit of help we can give. If we only have week, we need to make the most of it."

"Quick, get your things, Viola," Emilia said. She moved towards the hallway. "I'll help you pack so you can beat the curfew. But we need to start now. Don't worry about Ebb. I will make sure she's looked after while you're gone."

"We'll wait for you down here," William said as Viola hurried out of the room after her mum.

****

"I'm sorry it's not the best space to sleep."

"Don't worry about it, Casey. You didn't need to let us stay here." William placed his bag on the left-hand side of the bed.

"Yeah, it will be cosy. Thank you for letting us take over your spare room." Viola pulled back the covers on the other side and moved the pillows.

"It's not like I'll be having any other guests round for a while."

"Who needs other guests when you have us two?"

"Yeah, my two *favourite* people living with me. For at least a week. Who else would I need to see or spend time with when I have you two? I *can't* imagine anything going wrong here."

William threw one of the pillows at her. "Would you rather you were alone?"

"Don't break my things."

"I promise to stay out of your way as much as possible," Viola said. "I know I'm not someone you thought would be living with you, and I don't want you to feel uncomfortable."

"It's fine. We're all adults here." Casey stepped through the doorway. "Sorry you have to bunk together. See you in the morning."

"Night," Viola called out to her.

"Will your beau mind you sharing a bed with such a dashing companion?" He winked at her as he settled himself onto his half.

"I'll let you know when I have to."

"Ouch. You know how to hurt a guy." He smiled as he held his hand above his heart.

"I'm sure you'll bounce back." She made sure that she couldn't catch his eye, or she would never keep the small laugh that threatened to bubble up at bay.

Viola rummaged through her bag and pulled out her blanket. She placed it in the small space available on the floor.

"What are you doing?" William asked as she placed herself in the centre of the spread.

"Shush, I need to concentrate."

Viola closed her eyes and called the energy to her. The familiar thrum rose to the surface. She pushed out carefully, feeling for anything in place around the house. After a few minutes, she was confident this house hadn't been targeted yet.

"That feels weird," William said, rubbing his arms.

"Sorry, but on the plus side, the house is clean. Now to set up my own protections."

"The house is clean? Protections?"

"Shush."

Viola screwed up her face as she worked her energy into the house. She ran through the basic protections she placed in all her needed spots. She finished with a small piece of protection that would soften the feeling of her energy on the house. It wasn't as precise as she'd have liked, but the time it would take wasn't a luxury they could afford.

She opened her eyes. William watched her from the bed. "I've been practising this a lot longer than you." She shrugged as she climbed onto the bed.

"I know, but I didn't realise how much." He sat in silence. "I could feel what you were doing. I've never seen or felt anyone use magic like that. No wonder the Elders don't want you using it too often. You could take over so easily."

"And be in charge of the coven? No, thank you." Viola pulled the covers over her. "I don't know why having the strength to do something means I would do it. I don't want that life. I want to keep people safe and live my own life without worrying what everyone else is doing."

"People fear what they know they can't stop." William shrugged. "It has to worry some people to know you could run rings around them."

"Let's hope I won't have to demonstrate the skills I have."

Chapter Twenty-Nine

"Guys, I think I've found something." Casey's eyes widened as she ran over the page again.

"What is it?" William asked, looking up from his own notebook.

Casey beckoned him and Viola as she flipped the notebook around. "Okay, so we know this is all about the people joining together, right?" Her fingers circled the now recognisable diagram.

"Your point being?" Viola rubbed her eyes, not seeing what excited Casey.

"The circle isn't sat inside. We've never thought about what that might be."

"Isn't it supposed to represent the people who have joined?" William asked.

"I thought it might be, but then I was thinking, why would you need to contain it in a picture? What else could be encircling them?"

"Please can you tell us; my brain is too fried to work it out," Viola said.

"The coven."

"The coven?"

"The coven," Casey said again. "When we go through the initiation, we're all linked. Not in the same way as we are, but it's how the coven stays strong. What if the spell uses that to keep the coven safe and also uses some of the magic from the people inside it? You wouldn't need to complete the joining we have, but you would have access to some of the energy."

"How have we missed this? This is huge." Viola said, quickly pulling the notebook closer to her.

"Who would have thought Alexander Everett was siphoning from people without their consent."

"I can't believe he would," Viola murmured. "Why would he need to?"

"Hey, we don't know for sure that's what he did." Casey tried to console her.

"No, but what else could it mean?"

"That there is something to do with the acceptance in the coven which is needed by the linked people. It doesn't mean he did anything wrong."

"Sometimes good people do bad things."

"Before you keep spiralling." William leaned over the table. "Does this mean we're asking the Elders for their help? If they refused Alex, and I'm guessing it was a refusal, I can't see how they would agree to working with us for it."

"We have proof it works now, and if they agree, we can find a way to keep it going indefinitely."

"I'm with Will. I don't think they will work with us. But we can ask and see how much they know. Or ask

Thomas if he knows what the Elders know about this."

Casey pursed her lips. "I can ask Ms. Glorian tomorrow. You two go and pester Thomas." She paused. "But don't force any answers from him."

"Check. No force to be used."

"I wasn't talking to you, Will."

"Fine. I promise to only ask and not push him to answer when he doesn't want to," Viola said.

"Good. He helped us with some information last time, so it should be easy."

"Perfect. I think after all the excitement from this," Viola gestured in front of her, "and the hospital, I'm going to crash. Maybe we will have this done before the end of the month."

****

William knocked on the door as Viola hung back. The sooner they could get some information, the better. The sun burned against them as they waited. After a few minutes, William knocked again.

"I don't think anyone's home."

Viola sighed. "Keep watch for a second."

William nodded as she placed her hand against the door frame. Her eyes fluttered closed, the familiar twinge of her energy skimming against its surface.

"It's clear. No magic left behind," she murmured. Her hand still lay against the plastic.

"Do you know if he's home?"

"Nope, but at least we know he's not trying to ignore anyone."

"We should come back later."

Viola dropped her hand and began to move down

the garden path when the door sounded behind them.

"Do those notebooks not tell you it's rude to read other people's protections?"

"Thomas, you're home," William said to cut off the reply Viola had started to say.

"I told you last time I wouldn't help you kill yourself, and you've dragged someone else to my house." Thomas folded his arms and stared at her.

"You already knew we were joined."

"And I told you to stop. Don't be like your dad."

"I'm not. I'm being myself."

"You won't get through to her, Tom. She doesn't listen to anyone."

Thomas narrowed his eyes at the nickname. "Great. As stubborn as Alex. Just what we need. Get inside before anyone sees you."

He led the way into the living room Viola had sat in before. He didn't say anything to them as he sat in the chair. He motioned to the sofa opposite him.

"Spill. What do you want?"

"We need to know the magic my dad was creating. More importantly, how he managed to create the protection," Viola started.

"The protection had to have some link to the coven, but we don't know how or what he did to complete it," William added.

"Alex was a genius, but he didn't always make the best decisions," Thomas said.

"So, he did create a link with the coven?" Viola sat back into the chair, trying to let its comfort stop her spiralling thoughts.

"No. He couldn't find a way to make it stick. He tried a few times, though."

"At least he didn't achieve something like that without everyone's consent." William looked across to her.

"Only because he died before he figured it out," Thomas said dryly.

Viola narrowed her eyes. "Did the Elders know what he was doing?"

Thomas nodded. "They didn't like the idea. They thought he was going too far; it didn't matter that Alex was trying to help everyone. I think it was pride. None of them had come up with the idea, so they didn't want to help anyone else do it. It's why I think Abigail was always so happy to paint you in a negative light. To try and stop anyone from helping you get further than him."

"I've heard I'm due to be taking over any day now." She sighed, her shoulders dropping at the confirmation of Thomas's statement. She'd known it deep down, but it was different hearing it confirmed by someone else.

"And we will all bow down to our benevolent dictator." William smiled at her. She tried to return his smile, appreciating the gesture, but she knew it didn't come out right.

"By the time Alex figured out another plan, he wouldn't tell anyone about it, not even the people who sided with him. I don't know what he did to get the magic to stick. All I know is he went out one night to put something in place and he lost his life the same night."

"He never said anything?"

"Not to me. And I'm guessing he didn't tell Emilia anything. He never wanted her to know. He thought she would worry too much if she realised how much he was trying to do. It's a wonder she still looks so young, what with you following too closely in your dad's footsteps."

Viola looked from his face, not wishing to see the judgement. "She said she never asked him so she could pretend it wasn't as dangerous as she thought." She pulled one of the cream cushions over her body. "No wonder she's always pretending to ignore what I'm doing."

"There's still time for you to stop this."

To Viola's surprise, William answered, "Unfortunately, we can't do that. The coven needs us, even if they don't want to accept it. And if no one wants to help us, then I guess we'll have to do it on our own."

Thomas sighed. "I can't help you how you want me to. But I can let you know one thing; it was something we struggled with. You need to make sure your magic is in sync. Practise what you can to make sure you have similar strengths and don't shy away from the way you're connected. It might save your lives."

Viola stared. "You felt it, didn't you?"

Thomas held her gaze. "We've all felt someone dying through the link. Usually, it's a small ripple, and a hint of sadness. This was a rupture. Alex was stronger and his energy called out to us, but we couldn't help. We nearly lost our own connections to the coven."

"Thanks, for what you could tell us," William said. He pulled back the hand that reached out to Thomas. "We'll leave you alone."

They stood and moved towards the front door. Before they left the room, Viola turned and placed a hand gingerly on his shoulder. She pushed some of her energy towards him, doing what she could to lessen the grief etched on his face.

"What? How?" Thomas's shock rippled back at her.

She placed a finger to her lips. "Thank you for doing what you could for him. And for trying to stop me from doing the same. I hope this can help you. No one should have to have that feeling stuck with them."

Thomas grabbed her fingers and gave the smallest squeeze before he released her. "Thank you. Alex would have been proud of the woman you've grown to be."

She scrunched up her face. "I've heard that a few times."

****

"It's a no go," Casey called through the house as the front door closed behind her. "Ms. Glorian wouldn't speak to me about it at all. She even reminded me to call her Ms. Glorian rather than Abigail." She fell into an empty chair. "I don't know what it is about this magic she doesn't like, but I think we'll have to decipher a little more and see if there's way to keep it going."

"If she's unwilling to speak to you, there's no hope for anyone getting it out of her." William sighed as he made his way over to her.

"We didn't get much from Thomas either," Viola added. "He wouldn't talk about any of the exacts of what Dad was doing, but he did say that there was never a link created with the coven. Not for lack of trying, though."

"So, we're back to square one?"

"Maybe not," William said. "I think I know how we can use this connection."

"Didn't you have work today?" Casey asked. She sat up straighter in the chair and stared at him.

"I don't know what you think working in an office is like, but it doesn't use that much brain power."

Viola snorted from across the room.

"What was that?" William looked at directly at her.

"Someone had to say it." Viola crossed her arms and held his stare, her mouth pulling up into a smile.

"Careful, Vi, or I might use some of my newfound magic on you."

"You could use the practice."

"Will, focus. Vi, shut up. What did you figure out?" Casey asked.

"The joining we did means we can pull each other's magic. We can follow it if we want to."

Casey and Viola nodded.

"I may have zoned out at work and started feeling out with that magic. It was only gentle, but I listened to its hum and then I picked up on a feeling under it."

"Under it?"

"Yes. No. I don't know. But I was able to pick up on something else. It's faint, but there was something else there. I took an early lunch and decided to follow it."

Casey leaned into him. "And?"

"I ended up in a bookshop not too far from work. Inside was Peter." He waited. "You know Peter. He's a few years older than us, initiated about five years ago." Both women retained their blank expressions. "Anyway, it was his magic, but I could still feel it. You were right about the initiation linking us. But it's so minimal so as to not be obvious."

"That could be why Ms. Glorian is being so cagey. If we figure out what's up and tell people about this."

"Why would the Elders keep this from us?"

"Beats me, but they have."

"That's not what I'm getting at." William shushed them. "We could use that extra link as a way to link the protection spell to the coven."

"Wait. We could anchor it to the coven link?" The possibilities of what they had stumbled on flashed through Viola's mind.

"If we can find a way to make it stick, yeah. Then no one else would have to go through all this again."

"And deprive future generations of these brain teasers?" Casey said, her face lighting up. "If this is true, you might have saved us." She pulled him to her and kissed his cheek.

William laughed. "Now I know you're ecstatic."

"This is huge, Will," Viola said. "I'll think of some ways we could link the magic while I'm on my way to David's."

"If you think of anything, let us know."

"Will do. Cover for me if anyone comes over and asks where I am." Viola shrugged her jacket over her shoulder. "I shouldn't be too long, but it would be my luck that we would have a surprise visit tonight."

Chapter Thirty

Viola fidgeted in her seat as she waited for David to return to the living room. He'd said he only had a quick call to make, but she was getting antsy at each passing minute. Curfew was inching closer, and she already didn't want to explain what she was doing out if she was caught. She waited a few moments more before impatience got the better of her. David's house was bigger than her own, and the few times she had been over, she hadn't had much of a chance to explore. She couldn't think of a time she had even had to venture upstairs. Her energy pushed against her; she let it blanket her out of habit.

Her fingertips skimmed across the wall as she moved down the hallway towards the stairs. Her steps faltered as a familiar sensation rippled back at her. She stilled. Retracing the line she had made moments before, she tried to push pass the blood pounding in her head. This wasn't something she had encountered here before, and she didn't want to believe what she had stumbled across. There was only one reason why that particular signature would be left in David's home, and she needed to prove she was wrong.

Her eyes darted around as she checked that David hadn't finished his phone call. She closed her eyes and pushed out the energy, feeling for the fissure as though it was her fingernail looking for the edge of the tape. It was subtle. Viola couldn't tell if the residue was old, or if whoever had done it had tried to hide it. She moved to stand in front of where she had felt the bump. Her fingers pressed against the wall, gliding across the surface. She couldn't find anything.

"I could be wrong," she muttered to herself.

Viola paused. If that was the same energy type from the hospital, then maybe she hadn't kept anyone safe from what she was. She didn't realise anyone outside of a select few even knew about her spending time with David. Unless he knew what she was. She shook the thought from her head. Impossible. Why wouldn't he have mentioned something before if he knew?

She splayed her fingers against the wall and pushed inwards. When she felt nothing give, she tried to grasp at the surface and pull it towards her.

"A-ha." Her fingers caught hold of a slight groove.

She looked around her once more before peering at the spot by her hand. It took a few seconds for her eyes to focus on a strange line within the pattern on the wall. It ran the full length from what she could see. She dug her fingers into the groove and pulled. The wall swung open easily toward her. Viola looked down the corridor. With no sign of David, she took a step into the room before her.

A gasp escaped her mouth at what she saw. One corner of the room was filled with pictures of not only her, but Casey, William, and her mum. There were a few people she didn't recognise, but it could have been other members of the coven. There were a few sticky notes placed on some of the pictures, but she was too far away to read what they had on them. The pictures had startled her, but the thing that chilled her was the symbol scrawled on a piece of paper. It matched the one found near Sophie's body.

She stumbled from the room and pushed the door closed behind her. Her heart thudded as she raced back into the living room. David still wasn't anywhere to be seen. The only blessing of his busy work life. She stopped, her thoughts racing as she decided what to do. Confront him, or warn the people closest to her. If she left, he knew where to find her, and from what she'd seen, he knew where to find all of them. She wouldn't be able to keep them safe if she didn't make it back to them.

She shrugged on her coat and had almost reached the front door when she heard his voice.

"…yes, I understand. Thank you for your time. Enjoy your evening." His voice grew louder with every word.

She took the final few steps she needed and bolted into the night.

****

"William, thank the stars you answered." Viola breathed down the phone. "You need to get home as soon as you can. If you can get in touch with Casey, make sure she ends up home as well."

"Slow down. What's wrong?"

"I don't have time to explain. I'll let you know as soon as I'm back inside. I need to know that you're both safe. Don't answer the door to anyone. If you can add any extra protection to the house, do it. I'll find a way to make it through and add more when I'm home."

"Viola, what is—"

She hung up the phone, shoving it into her pocket, and picked up her pace. She'd run through the gardens to avoid being seen by anyone driving a car. The cold night air pierced at her skin, but she used the sensation to push her rather than slow her down. She knew she wouldn't be able to run or walk the entire way back to Casey's. She could have caught a bus, or ordered a taxi, but she didn't want to be somewhere she could be easily found. Or at least somewhere David would know where to look for her.

Viola pulled her phone from her pocket and sent a quick text to her mum. That was another place she didn't want David turning up to. When she had a minute, she would phone her mum and explain what she could.

✳✳✳✳✳✳✳✳✳✳✳✳

Relief flooded through Viola as she saw Casey's house coming into view. As she reached the front door, she felt for any additional protection in place. There was a slight resistance to her prodding, and she was glad they had taken her seriously. She pushed her way into the house and locked the door behind her.

Viola collapsed against the door, the safety of the house allowing all her emotions to fall out of her. She struggled to catch her breath as her body shook with her sobs.

"Viola!" Casey called, pulling her into a hug. "It's okay. You're going to be okay," she cooed against her head.

"Hey, Vi. What was the phone call about?" William shouted through the house.

"Not now, Will," Casey called back. She turned back to Viola. "Do you think you can get up and make it to the sofa?"

Viola nodded between the shuddering of her body as Casey helped her stand.

"Will, we need tea and blankets," Casey said as she led Viola into the other room.

Viola tried to pull herself together. To slow the tears and calm the distress that racked through her body. She pulled the proffered green blanket around her shoulders. Wrapped in the warmth and comfort of safety, she succeeded in calming down.

"Do you mind telling us what that was all about?" Casey asked, sitting next to her on the sofa.

"I think I know who took the witches and who killed Sophie," Viola said.

"Wait, what?"

Viola nodded. "I think it was David."

"The guy you're seeing?"

Viola nodded again, tears building up in her eyes. "You were right, Casey. It's all my fault this is happening." Her voice broke at the end. Reality fell on her like an over-stacked bookshelf toppling.

"Will, we might need something stronger than tea,"

Casey shouted.

Steps thudded into the living room. "What did I miss? Why is tea not strong enough?" Will looked between the two women.

"I think David is the witch hunter, and I brought him to us," Viola said, the words hanging in the room.

"Where's the wine?" Will asked.

"Cupboard by the fridge," Casey answered.

"I think he was tracking me. He had all these pictures up on the wall, and there were some with you and Will. I'm so sorry. I didn't realise. I shouldn't have brought you two into this." Her self-pitying tirade slowed. She turned to Casey, grabbing her hand. "That's how he knew where to find me the other night."

"He found you?"

"When I stormed off. I didn't even know where I'd gone, but he appeared out of nowhere. I didn't think anything was off. I was happy to have someone to talk to. I can't believe I let this happen."

"Hey, it's not your fault someone thinks it's okay to go around killing others because they're different from them. We'll make sure he can't hurt anyone else."

Viola nodded as Will passed her a tumbler filled with wine.

"Sorry. I couldn't find the proper glasses."

"It's fine." She took a drink. "I didn't realise I needed that."

"So, he was tracking you?" Will asked.

"Tracking or stalking. I'm not sure which. But it makes sense. I run into him, and suddenly, Sophie goes missing. Then the weird issue at the hospital. How did I not see it before?"

"Why would you?" Casey said. "Do we have to vet every new person we meet? I've never looked at someone on the street and wondered if they were a serial killer in disguise. It's not your fault you trusted someone. Trusting people is a good thing."

"Most people don't trust someone who is trying to bring about the end to their way of life," Viola mumbled into her glass.

"Enough people trust those they shouldn't. You aren't the first, and unfortunately, you won't be the last."

"I feel like such an idiot."

"We're all idiots when it comes to love. Don't let that be your bar for the future."

"She's right, Viola. One bad guy doesn't make us all like that." William tried to cheer her up.

A buzzing against Viola's leg distracted her from the conversation. She pulled the phone from her pocket to see her mum's name flash across the screen.

"Mum, are you okay?" Violas asked.

"Yes, I'm fine. How are you? Where are you? Your text made no sense. What happened with David?"

"Mum, I think he's the witch hunter."

"What?" Emilia's voice dropped her usual light tone. If it hadn't been Viola speaking to her, she might have missed the hint of fear that laced the word.

Viola filled her in on the last couple of hours of her day. She tried to quell the wave of emotion rising through her as she relived it again. "I think I led him to us."

"Did you speak to him about it?"

"No, I left before I saw him. I didn't know what to say."

"Did your magic have any reactions to him?"

"I, it, I mean. I might have had a few sparks. Electric shocks when I touched him. My energy seemed to hum when I was with him."

"Interesting."

The pause stretched on between them. Casey and William looked between themselves as Viola checked the call hadn't dropped.

"Mum, are you still there?"

"Yes. I'm thinking." Emilia sighed. "Stay where you are and don't try to come here for a couple of days. I'll do what I can to keep the house secure, but you need to do what you can to keep us all safe."

"I'm not leaving you there on your own. You can come here." Viola looked across to Casey, who nodded back at her.

"No. You don't need me getting in the way. You three need to keep going and get this working. I believe in you all."

The phone beeped in her ear. Viola looked in disbelief at the black screen. Maybe the stubborn part of her wasn't from her dad.

"She's staying there," Viola said.

"It'll be okay, Vi. We'll make sure she's safe." Casey reached across and squeezed her shoulder.

"You must be feeling sorry for me," Viola said. "A nickname and physical contact."

"Don't get used to this." Casey smiled at her.

"I think we might need to finish off this wine," Will said, getting up from his seat and heading back into the kitchen.

Casey worried her lip. "We need to contact Abigail. I know we don't want that conversation hanging over us, but she needs to know. It might help if we have an idea of at least one of the people watching us."

"You don't think David is working alone?"

"Hunters rarely work alone. I don't know if that's still the case, but we can't rule it out."

****

"Viola," his voice called for her as she left the bus.

She pushed her shoulders back and continued towards the hospital. A hand grabbed her arm, pulling her off balance into the body behind her. She flinched away from him as her energy tried to pull her closer. Her head whipped round.

"Viola, I've been trying to get in touch with you."

"I know."

David stood, his hand still around her arm. "I thought something was wrong. You disappeared the other night."

"Something came up." She pulled at his grasp.

"Something came up so you've had to ignore me?" He let go of her, and Viola hated that there was a part of her that missed his touch.

"Work's been busy, and there's been some stuff going on that needed my attention."

"Vi, come on. Talk to me."

"I'm sorry, David. I don't think this is going to work out." The words tumbled from her mouth. "I don't have time for whatever we are. This could never work out. We're too different, and we need to stop pretending that we aren't."

"Don't say that."

Viola finally looked at his face. His eyes pleaded

with her. Her resolve wavered until the thoughts of Sophie and Evie came back to her. "I have to go. You're making me late."

He took a step back, his eyes shining. "I can't have that." He smiled without the warmth reaching his eyes. "If you change your mind or need another friend, you know where to find me."

"Goodbye, David."

She took a couple of steps backward before she turned and continued on her way to work.

****

"He came to your place of work?"

"Yes, I've been avoiding him. I didn't think he would do something like that." Viola chewed at her lip, and she fished the notebook from her bag.

"You going to be okay? I can get the bus with you if it will make you feel safer," William offered.

"I'll be fine. I don't think he knows how strong I am." She flipped the book to one of the pages towards the end. "This is my own work; I've been adding in everything I've experimented on and how it's gone." She turned it around so her friends could see. "This is the last thing I worked on before going through my dad's things."

Casey peered at the ink-scrawled page. "You mended a cup?"

"No, look," Viola said, running a finger under one line.

"Wow, you managed to use magic that wasn't your own." William stared at her. "Can I be your grand vizier when you take over the coven?"

"How did you manage that?" Casey mumbled, pulling the notebook toward her. "...cup while meditating. Meditating? You did this when recharging?"

"I was fed up with fainting all the time."

Casey pinched her nose. "Of course that's something you deal with."

"Not for a while, but I've not had much chance to practise it."

William pulled the book from Casey. "I joke a lot, Vi, but this is really impressive. If a little worrying. I didn't realise you were this powerful. There's never been another recorded instance of someone pulling off something like that."

"Maybe they didn't want anyone to know about it." Viola waved them off. "But that's not important. I wanted a fail-safe, something I could pass onto the coven. Then, if someone felt like they were getting too close to the edge of their abilities, there would be something they could fall back on. I thought it would be helpful, but when we realised what my dad had stumbled on, I searched this out."

"It could be the same thing he was looking into." Casey sat back in her chair.

"If he knew he could connect into the coven's power, it might be that he was doing this," William admitted. "But it's doubtful. If he could do that, then he should have found a way to survive the protection being placed."

"Unless he didn't know how to keep it going." Casey took the notebook back and flipped through some pages. "Maybe it was still too much for one person to endure. But it might save one of our lives."

"You think?"

"Maybe. I would feel more confident if Will and I were at the same level as you, but I don't think we're going to have the time to improve that much." Casey gave a wry smile.

"Speak for yourself. I feel like I'm an adept student." William flexed his arms at them.

"Not helping." Viola laughed. "Casey's right, we won't have much longer to get this figured out. We have no how idea when David might act."
William pulled his phone out of his pocket and quickly typed on the screen. "We have two weeks to be ready. The next new moon will have to be the one that we make this work."

Viola didn't respond to him but there was a shift in the room. They all felt the weight of what they were about to do and they wouldn't have the luxury of making any mistakes with it. If they couldn't fix this now, they would leave everyone open to being found.

Chapter Thirty-One

"Try it again," Viola said.

Casey took a deep breath. Her eyes closed as she shook her arms. The vibrations pulled at Viola as the other woman concentrated on her energy.

"Listen to my voice. Try not to let it annoy you."

"That will be difficult," Casey mumbled, but Viola saw the smile on her face.

"Focus on the energy. Feel it bubble just beneath the skin, threatening to break out." Viola mimicked Casey's breathing, her own energy responding to her words. "Let it skim across the skin, but don't release it."

Casey scrunched up her face. "How do you do this all the time?"

"Practice. Now, keep hold of it. Can you feel it on your hands?"

"I'm not sure."

"Move your fingers. There should be a little delay. If you can't feel a difference, then we need to practise a little more."

Casey flexed her fingers. "No, I can't feel anything but my fingers." She sighed.

"No, don't give up. Try again."

Casey took another breath. Her face relaxed as she let the energy gather around her.

"You need to let it cover you. Imagine the energy is a piece of clothing, but it's covering your entire body."

"You're making this harder," Casey muttered.

"Okay, let's try this instead. Watch." Viola spread out her arms, willing her energy to the surface. It didn't take much encouragement, her own magic responding to her usual pull. She focused on the feeling and worked to give it a shimmer across her skin. "Did you feel what I did?"

Casey shook her head. "No. I mean, yes. I could feel you pulling at it, but I couldn't feel how you did it."

"Can you at least see what I've done?"

"Yeah. The glitter effect was a nice touch. Although, weird to see it all over."

"That's one thing, then. Now, you try it."

"Try what?"

"The glitter. Pull your magic to your skin and tweak it so I can see. It will give us an idea of how easily it's responding to you."

Viola focused on Casey. Small flecks of stars flashed across the woman's skin.

"You're doing great." Viola couldn't keep the smile from her voice. After a few minutes, Casey's skin twinkled back at her. "Open your eyes."

A small squeak left her body. "I did it."

"Don't be so shocked. You're a natural. Next, understanding how to feel out with your magic."

They spent the better part of two hours going over basic techniques on how to channel the energy around them and create a protective barrier. It wouldn't be the same as the full protection the coven needed, but they all needed to be at their strongest so they could get it to work. By the end of the session, Casey was able to easily pull her energy to her and also search out for where other spells had been anchored. Viola felt exhausted by the end of it, but she was proud of how far they had been able to come.

Once Casey left the room, Viola flicked back to her notes and jotted down a few things from the session. If they could find their own strengths, they would be able to use it to their advantage if anything were to happen. Viola pondered at the way her life had changed. Last year, she never would have imagined sitting in Casey's house, never mind temporarily living there. It felt nice to have others to talk to about what she was doing, and she only hoped the imminent danger wasn't the only reason they were becoming as close as they were. She hurried to put her notes away as she heard the doorbell ring, signalling the arrive of food.

****

William stuffed his face with the slice of pizza he was holding. "Practice gone well?" he asked between mouthfuls.

"Great."

"Terrible."

Casey and Viola spoke at the same time.

"Okay, maybe not great," Viola conceded. "But we made a lot of progress."

"I don't think we will be ready in time to complete the magic."

"The least we can do is try."

"You'll get the hang of it in no time, Case," William said.

"Don't forget about you," Casey said.

"Wait, what?" William swallowed the last bite of cheesy carbs.

"We all need to be ready, so you can't expect it to fall on our shoulders," Viola said as she took a slice of pizza.

"But there won't be enough time to train both of us. I thought my power would be from working out where we need to complete the protection spell."

"You can do both."

"Yeah, Will. It will be good for you to get out of your comfort zone." Casey laughed as she poured water into her glass. "We can experience the wonders of Viola's teaching methods together."

"You say that as if you're not enjoying yourself," Viola said.

"You think being patronised is fun?"

"I do *not* do that."

"Maybe it's not a conscious thing."

"You could have said something earlier." Viola lowered her voice before eating another slice.

"I'm sure you're a great teacher, Vi," William said.

"I've not even tried to help you yet. Don't start on me as well."

They laughed at her, but Viola couldn't help but

join in.

"Okay, so we are getting stronger, and we still haven't had anyone come to the house to put dampeners on it." Viola checked the date on her phone. "That gives us a few days still, and the next new moon isn't for another week. If we can try and be ready for then, we might have a chance. Will, are you any closer to finding us the location? I know we think the protection can be added into the coven link, but I still think we need a place we're linked to. It should give us the strongest connection to the coven to get the placement right."

He shook his head. "No. No one has mentioned anything about a sacred spot to the coven, and I've not been able to find anywhere that has a highly concentrated amount of energy."

Viola tried to hide her frustration. "It's okay. We've still got time."

"You don't need to pretend you're not annoyed," Casey said. "We can tell. And I don't know about Will, but I'm annoyed as well. If anyone else was willing to help, we wouldn't be having to muddle through this mess. We're doing the best we can, and so are you."

"Thanks. It means a lot." Viola smiled at her. "I feel like we're running out of time and we'll be too late to stop someone else from being hurt."

Chapter Thirty-Two

The heaviness of the room settled on her. She felt like she was suffocating from the impending conversation.

"You said you had an urgent matter about which to speak to me," Ms. Glorian said.

"Yes," Viola said. The silence dropped over them again.

"I know of your meddling with the protection spell. If it's anything to do with that, I hope it is good news."

"No, it's about the missing people." Viola fiddled with the edge of her grey cardigan. "I think I might know who is behind it, but I need to explain how I know."

Ms. Glorian didn't say anything but continued to look at her.

"You're aware that each spell, and each person, has their own unique signature."

The Elder inclined her head.

"I may have been honing that skill over the past few years. Attempting to understand the work being done, and how to identify who might have done what." The only response was a slight raising of Ms. Glorian's eyebrow. "I think I know who placed the magic in the hospital. The magic that was looking out for someone who also used magic."

"Did I not tell you to stay away from that?"

"Yes, but I remembered how it felt."

"Viola, I will not sit here and listen to you tell me about the ways you have violated the coven rules."

"No, *Abigail,* that's not what I've done. I think I know who we need to target to keep the coven safe. I couldn't do much to unravel the magic placed there without tipping them off, but I know it was the same."

"Unravelling someone else's magic?" Ms. Glorian's face was ashen. "You are not to speak of those skills with anyone else in the coven. And while I discuss with the other Elders, you are not permitted to further any of your research into the protection spell. We need people who are not looking to further their own ambitions helping this coven."

"Their own what?" Viola felt the polite smile slip from her face. "Are you not listening to me? I think I might know who killed Sophie and who might have taken Evie, and all you hear is that I'm trying to further some sort of ambition. *Everything* I do is for this coven."

"I think it would be best if you left." Ms. Glorian stood from the armchair.

"Gladly. I hope you and the council enjoy your discussions going nowhere. When you realise you need me, don't bother." Viola stormed from the room but made sure the front door closed softly behind her. She wouldn't give her the satisfaction of telling the others how Viola Everett slammed the door in a tantrum.

****

"Are you sure she meant it like that?" William asked.

"Yep, so I guess you've been right all along." Viola leaned against the sofa. "She's been waiting for me to make some sort of power grab, and as soon as I mentioned unravelling magic, she kicked me out."

"You are pretty badass, but I didn't think she would be so easily spooked."

"It will be the protection," Casey said, not looking up from her book. "She knows we don't have much time left to resolve it. She'll be worried that anyone who knew what Alex did, or who could figure it out, might be able to do something to oust her from her position. Not that I think that's what you're going to do, Vi. At least, not anymore."

"Thanks. It's nice to know that all these months have had some impact."

"Look at my two girls finally getting on." William leaned over to muss both of their hair.

Viola threw a cushion at him. "I can turn my annoyance onto you if you want."

"No, thanks. I do not want to be on the receiving end of your anger." He scratched his head. "But if she didn't listen to you, what do we do now?"

"What we've been doing all along. Keeping the coven protected."

"And David?"

"We can deal with him when we know everyone

else should be safe. I don't want to do something too rash and find out that we can't stop anyone else from being able to find us."

"I do believe we've rubbed off on you. No rushing into your emotions. You make me proud."

"Don't make me throw another cushion."

"So, we carry on as normal?" Casey asked.

"It's the only thing we can do," Viola said. "If we can crack the final piece of the puzzle, we can get this over with once and for all."

Chapter Thirty-Three

"Watch me," Viola said.

She focused on the energy, infusing it with more of a shimmer so Casey and William could see what she was doing, rather than her usual method. The wisps twinkled in front of her. She concentrated, moving them towards the wall.

"I'm going to find the pressure point from the soundproofing spell. Imagine you're finding the end of the sticky tape on the roll with your fingernail. You can't see it, but you'll feel a slight ridge. I'm hoping you'll be able to see what I'm doing."

The energy ran against the surface. It rippled as it hit the soundproofing spell. She pushed the energy into a narrower strip. The ripple increased as she ran it back across the spot.

"How long have you been able to do that?" William

asked as he took a step closer to the wall, his hand twitching to reach out.

"A few years." Viola shrugged. "It's useful if you want to find something." She moved slightly closer to the spot her magic identified. "Now, we're going to break the soundproofing."

"Break the magic?" Casey asked. "You can break the magic as well? The magic you didn't place or create." She sank to the floor.

"Do we want to figure out how to put this protection back or not?" Viola asked, focusing on her magic so it didn't slip.

"Yes, we do," William said. "But this seems too advanced. We're not going to be undoing what your dad did. We don't know where he anchored it." He paused. "Does anyone else know that you're able to do this?"

Viola shook her head. "I've never mentioned it. I mean, my mum might have picked up on some things, but we don't sit and talk about the magic we've been using. I think she might have a heart attack if she knew everything I do with it. Also, we might not need to undo anything, but if you can understand what's happening, it might help you improve on what you're capable of."

"Have I ever told you how much I love you?" William asked, stepping closer to her and squeezing her arm.

"Knock it off. I'm not going to hurt you." Viola huffed. "If I wanted to, I'd have done so already."

"Glad to know you don't wield your powers for evil."

"If I did, the coven would be a lot safer." Viola

stared at the other two. "But as I'm not, I'll try and show you." She focused back on the wall. "All magic has its own signature, and for some reason, it's almost like a knot is formed at the pinnacle of it. The part keeping it together. If you can break the knot, you let the magic fall from where it's been placed. If you know who's placed it there, it can be easier to undo."

"So, it's like a wine stopper?" William asked.

Viola frowned. "I guess so. I never thought of it that way, but it is a stopper."

"Can you tell how they got the magic to work?"

"I've not had the chance to look into it, but it could be another path for my study on it."

She picked at the magic, pulling on more of her strength to break the binding. Her tongue pushed against the top teeth as her energy plucked and picked at the embedding. This one must have been in place for a while as she found herself pulling deeper into her reserves.

"Viola," Casey said, her words slurred.

"What?" Viola asked, her eyes never leaving the spot.

"What... are... you... doing?"

"Like I said, I'm pulling at this to show you how to break someone else's work."

"Then... why... do... I... feel... so—"

Viola stopped what she was doing as Casey's body slumped to the floor. Viola rushed to her side, fingers pressed against her wrist. "Casey, can you hear me?"

"What happened?" William asked, sinking down Casey's other side.

"She's fainted," Viola said, her voice quiet. She pulled at William's arm. "Did you feel anything?"

"When?"

"When I was trying to break away the magic. Did you feel anything?"

"I felt a tug, but nothing much."

"I didn't feel anything. How could I not realise?" She wrapped her arms around her body.

"Hey, it's not your fault," William said, placing his hand on her arm. "It's not happened before. Why would we expect something like this to happen? At least we have another idea why Abigail has been so against it."

"If she knew this could happen, why didn't she warn us? We could have tried to prepare for it."

A silence lapsed over them. Viola moved and picked up Casey's arm. The steady rhythm of the unconscious woman's heartbeat soothed the erratic one holding her.

"How long will she be out for?" William asked.

Viola shrugged. "It depends on how used you are to using your energy."

"Should we move her somewhere more comfortable?"

"We can try. I'll grab her arms, and we can lift her onto the sofa."

Viola's fingers held onto her wrist. "Her heart rate is stable at least. Or it's not beating frantically."

"Is that a good thing or not?"

"I'll let you know," she mumbled.

"Is there a way to wake her up?"

With her free hand, Viola ran her fingers through her hair and wrapped the ends around her fingertips. "I don't know. Normally, I have to wait to wake up. It's the magic trying to keep you from draining completely. At least, that's my theory," she added quickly as William stared at her.

"If it's magic related, can't we give her some of ours? We're linked and we don't have to give her everything."

"Will, you're a genius." She leaned over and pulled his hand into hers. "Take hold of Casey's other arm."

"Okay, now what?"

"Close your eyes. We need to meditate and channel what we can into the link we have. It might not work, but if we can pull from each other along that line, we should be able to push as well."

Viola's eyes drifted closed as she allowed her energy to replenish. She searched for the connection between her and Casey. Her thoughts directed the energy along the thread, pushing strength into the unconscious woman at her side. As she felt William's energy join hers, Casey's pulse quickened under her thumb. She jerked her hand away and opened her eyes as she pulled William back with her.

"You can use your words you know," he said, rubbing at his wrist.

"Sorry. I'm still getting used to working with others."

"I'm guessing it worked?"

"I think so. Her pulse sped up and I didn't want to overload her." Viola sighed. "Now, we wait."

"I'll get us a drink."

"Sure."

****

Silence wrapped around them. Only silence. No clocks

ticking down the seconds or sounds of life sounding from outside the space. Their warm drinks cooled, untouched in their hands, the only hint they had been waiting longer than an hour. Viola focused on the unconscious woman in front of her, not wanting to do anything until she knew Casey was okay. Her usual fidgeting was gone as she kept watch. She couldn't be sure how long she sat there, but it was beginning to feel like days.

A sigh passed through them. Viola twisted at the sound. Casey moved, her unconscious state switching to more sleep-like behaviour. Viola stilled as she waited for her friend to wake up.

"Casey?" Viola said, her voice paper-thin, uncertain.

Casey's eyes opened and slowly looked around the room. Her hand rubbed at her temple. "What happened?" she croaked.

"We learnt why the coven is so against any of us joining our powers," Viola said.

"You had us worried there for a minute," William said.

"You pulled from me?" Casey asked as she pulled herself into a sitting position. She didn't sound angry, more confused.

Viola nodded. "I think I did, but I didn't realise. It didn't feel like it was coming from you. I'm so sorry, Casey. I promise I will be more careful in future so it doesn't happen again. Can you remember anything?"

Casey rubbed at her arm. "I was trying to pay attention to what you were doing. I might have opened myself up a little too much. It might not have been your fault. We should practise like that, to make sure we can withstand a little more strenuous usage." A wry smile crossed her face. "It might be a crash course on energy regeneration. How long was I out for?"

"Less than two hours—"

"About an hour and half—"

William and Viola spoke at the same time.

"That seems… fast."

"We used a life hack," William offered.

"If we can pull from each other, we can pass it back. You only fell unconscious to help speed it up. We nudged it along." Viola paused. "It was William who thought of it. I don't know how long you'd have been out otherwise."

"Thank you." Casey looked between them before staring at Viola. "I'm glad you don't use your powers for evil."

"I might if you keep pushing me."

Casey laughed before a coughing fit took over her.

"You okay?" Viola asked, discarding her cup to kneel in front of her.

"I'm fine, just weak. You don't need to check me over." Casey shook Viola's hand from her wrist.

"She seems good." William laughed.

"If we're all okay, maybe we should continue with our practice."

Chapter Thirty-Four

Viola flicked through one of her dad's notebooks. Her back was pressed against the wall as she sat on the borrowed bed, the notebook splayed across her folded legs. She skimmed through the pages, not taking in any of the information.

There wasn't much time left. They could all feel the protection fading. Even with everyone's life at stake, she couldn't understand what her dad had been writing. She hadn't seriously read through the notebooks for a while, the habit lingering long after the action was of use. If only there was a way to understand what might have been done. A way to work it all out.

Her eyes passed over a page she'd read hundreds of times before. This time, a single sentence jumped out at her. A sentence on its own in the middle of a page. It infuriated her today as much as it had when she first saw it. Despite the annoyance, she knew it had to be important. Would her dad have left a sentence on its own?

"What do you mean, Dad? Why did you write your notes like this?"

Connection sacrifices for the many.

He had made sure to leave this with gaps all around it. The lines above and below were empty. That was what infuriated her the most. Every other piece of white space had been filled in these books, but not this section. It couldn't have screamed, 'I'm more important' than if he'd written that next to it instead. The only problem was, she couldn't figure out why this one had to stand out so much.

"How can a connection be sacrificed? What sort of sacrifice could be done that would be for the many?" She tapped the open book against her head as she spoke. "Come on, Dad. You had to have left more of an idea than that. I know it's important."

She shifted on the bed, pulling the blanket around her shoulders and hugging her knees to her chest. She mumbled the sentence under her breath. "If we have a connection, we have to sacrifice it to help the many." Viola gasped. Her thoughts rushing over themselves at what she had stumbled across.

She finished transferring her thoughts to a fresh page when her phone vibrated in her pocket. At the name from the text, she almost threw her phone down until she read the preview of the message. Her hand shook as she unlocked the screen and read what David had sent her.

I know you've been looking for Evie. Meet at 7pm at the community centre. You know the one. Come alone.

Her heart stilled. He knew why she had been avoiding him. She glanced at the time on her phone. Six thirty p.m. She had enough time to get there but not much else. It took her a second to decide. She wouldn't endanger anyone else, not if she knew how to keep everyone safe. She felt her energy and searched for the other two. Their lines felt distant. There wasn't enough time for them to make it back and make a difference, but she knew she couldn't take off without letting them know.

Her fingers danced across the screen as she wrote her reply. No need for any unnecessary casualties if she could let him know she was on her way. She quickly flicked to the group chat and let them know she was going. She didn't tell them where, but this way, they would have an idea of what was happening. She hadn't had the chance to let them know what she had realised about her dad's work, so she sent as much of a summary as she could as she raced to get ready.

William tried to call her after he'd read her message, but she ignored him. She didn't have the mental capacity to deal with his pleading. She needed to go. Something was telling her that if she didn't meet him now, there would be worse consequences for them all. She sent another message telling them that her phone would be on silent and she wouldn't be able to respond to them, but she would try and let them know what she was doing and where she was through her connection to them. It wasn't a lot, but it would have to be enough.

Chapter Thirty-Five

The building was dark as Viola approached. She tentatively made her way to the entrance. Her heart thudded in her chest. She fought off the panic. She'd turned her phone to silent but had tugged with her energy to let Casey and William know to keep a feel for her. It might not be enough to keep her safe, but at least they would know where to find her.

She grasped the handle and didn't know if she wanted the door to be locked and this to be a crude joke. The door moved beneath her hand. With only a small pause to listen, she stepped into the darkened hallway.

The door closed behind her. "You can do this," she whispered to herself, unsure who she was trying to convince.

The familiar layout out of the centre disconcerted her. She didn't come here often, but she struggled to link the idea that a witch hunter was inside. This had always been a safe space for coven members. At least, it had been protected to be a safe space. She stilled. Maybe this was what she needed. She shuddered at the thought of David inside, desecrating that safety. This would be her final chance to keep everyone else safe. The silence stayed with her, no sign that anyone else was here other than the unlocked door. Her footsteps echoed as she walked the wooden floor to the back of the room. A frown formed on her face as she considered her options. If she were to host a hostage exchange, where would she do it?

"Hello?"

She moved to the staff only door that led to the stairs to the upper level. Downstairs was too open for anything clandestine to happen. Her fingers traced across the door and she paused. Viola let her energy feel out for any trap. There was an almost imperceptible ripple against her touch. She shuddered. It didn't feel deadly, but it confirmed to her that someone had hidden something upstairs out of the way. She scrunched up her fists as she steeled herself from what she was about to find.

The door pushed open silently. She paused again. The only sound she heard was that of her heart thrumming beneath her chest. A few slow steps brought her to the foot of the stairs. Common sense told her to leave and not walk into whatever trap David had left for her. Her hand hovered over the banister. Would she risk herself to get answers? Viola felt for her connection to Casey and William again. Their threads came easily to her. She tried to pass through her feelings of urgency and caution. If things went south, she hoped they would understand that they couldn't rush in and they'd find any back up.

Her mind set, she took the stairs two at a time. A breeze greeted her as she reached the landing. She followed it towards one of the rooms she hadn't been in before. The door stood ajar. The room was enshrouded in darkness. Viola couldn't feel the breeze any more, but she could feel something else pulling her towards this room.

"Hello, Viola. I see you listened to my text."

"David?" His voice didn't seem right; crueller than usual.

Laughter mocked her confusion. "No, not David. I will never understand what made him fixate on you."

A figure stepped towards her. It took a moment to recognise the man in front of her, the light from the streetlamps outside the only source of illumination. "Matthew?" David's father was not who she had expected to meet. "You brought me here? Why?"

"I would have thought that would be clear. I need you here to stop you from meddling with affairs that don't concern you."

Thoughts whirred through her mind.

"Did you know he was protecting you?" Matthew sneered.

His gesture caused her to look to his side. David stood behind his father, hidden within the shadows of the room. "What?" Viola asked, looking between the two men. "I've not had anyone protecting me."

Matthew tutted. "So conceited to think you could stay out of my radar on your own." He half-turned his head towards his son. "Was that part of her allure?"

David refused to meet her gaze, his head turned down towards the floor.

"Yes. My pathetic son thought he could keep you and your friends safe. He thought with his presence, I wouldn't find out what you are. Or where you were."

Viola flinched at the intensity of his words. "Why would he do that when he's a witch hunter?"

Matthew laughed, the cold, bitter sound frosting the air. "No, my dear. He's never approved of the way the family operates. He's rebelled since we told him of it. Not that he's ever openly defied me as much as this before." His eyes narrowed. "You must have quite some magic to make him drop all common sense."

The room spun around her. "No. He was trying to find out who we were. How to gain access to the entire coven and take us all out. He took those people."

Matthew sneered again. "You think David was responsible for this? You think he would be man enough to cause all these issues, to do what needs to be done?" He laughed, the sound dark and mocking. "Poor, foolish Viola. David has been trying to help you all this time. He's been keeping an eye on you to make sure you're safe. To try and hide you from me. Not that it helped him." He rounded on his son. "How did your attempts to create a distraction work for you? Now, I'll get to do what I'd planned before your interference."

David's head snapped up. He stared at his father, hatred laced across his brow. "I swear if you touch her, I'll—"

"You'll do what? We both know your threats are empty. You can't help anyone. Even after snooping around the house, you weren't able to help those I'd taken."

"You took them?" Viola said, her voice barely above a whisper, but he still heard her.

"Of course I did. The world needs to be rid of your filth. Our family has been hunting witches for centuries. Only, David thought he was better than it. Thought he could reason with me. I've never been so disappointed to have him as my son."

Viola looked between them; the hatred matched on both sides. With confirmation that it was Matthew who was responsible for the terrors inflicted on her coven, and that of the High Peak coven, her magic stirred. The familiar hum flickered beneath her fingers. After a moment, she felt a surge of energy as Casey and William opened up themselves to her.

She wove the energy over her, creating a thin barrier between her and the two men in front of her. Her concentration hadn't been noticed, as she began to weave the energy together again, this time knotting it as she had seen in her dad's book. She tried to remember which day the new moon was. She couldn't remember if it was tonight or tomorrow. It would have to do.

"How did you do it?" she asked, her voice threatening to break. "How did you find them?"

Matthew regarded her. "It was simple. Not all witches believe they should be allowed to live in peace. Some of you recognise the filthy abominations that you are. They created a gap for me to do what I do best. Even with the detection barrier in place, you can be found."

"One of our own helped you?" Repulsion rushed through her. "Why would anyone help you?"

"You are not all one people. Maybe you should be more friendly with each other rather than vying for power. It's pathetic. Like insects thinking they're in charge. Your hubris would always be your downfall."

Viola couldn't understand what he was saying. The words made sense, but there was no reason any witch would want the others brought down. How could you trust a witch hunter? There would be nothing stopping them from turning on you. No, she wouldn't believe it was someone who had been willing to help. There had to be more to it than that.

"There isn't anyone who would turn their backs on us. Everyone knows not to trust a hunter," she spat.

"Perhaps, but I have had help."

David narrowed his eyes at his dad. "How could you use her?"

"What?" Viola asked, her eyes focusing on David. "What is it?"

"Georgina," David said.

"Your sister?" A brief flash of a conversation they had had a few months ago rose to the surface of her mind.

He nodded.

"Your own daughter is a witch, and you still try to kill us." Her eyes widened.

"She knows her place, and she knows her power means nothing. Your power means nothing." Their was a glint of hatred in his eyes and a cruel edge to his tone.

He might be accepting of his daughter for what she could do for him, but she wasn't spared from his ire. Viola knew that without him having to say it. And she worried about the life Georgina had been forced into. Even if she had worked against her own kind, no one should have to live with someone telling them they were less than for something they couldn't change.

"You're delusional." Her heart thudded in her ears. What kind of person would use their daughter like that? Viola worried she wouldn't be able to reason with him. It wouldn't matter if she survived the spell, as she didn't believe she would be leaving this building alive.

"Practical. If the world wishes to inflict me with an abomination for a child, I will find a purpose for them."

"You promised you would keep her safe," David yelled, his frustration straining his voice. "That was part of the deal."

"She is safe. This world will be a safer place once I rid it of your girlfriend's kind."

"Viola, look out."

Her body was pushed to the side as her ears rang at the explosive noise. Dazed, she looked at Matthew. He stood, his arm raised, with a gun pointing where she had been seconds before. Where David's body now stood.

"David." The name ripped from Viola's mouth as his body collapsed in on itself.

She rushed to his side, feeling for his heartbeat. The barely-there stutter under her fingertips pushed aside some of her fear. It wasn't a lot, but it was enough. Blood already covered his shirt, the dark colour oozing from the wound to his stomach. She diverted some of her energy from the protection she was weaving and pulled it towards David's body. She slowly fed it into the wound and tried to stem some of the damage.

"Hold on," she whispered as she turned to face his attacker, her body angled between them.

Matthew regarded her. His eyes were hungry. Viola's fury twisted with her magic. The man in front of her had concocted everything. He'd been behind the death of two witches. How many other people had he killed? It didn't matter.

"I have to say, you are a lot fiercer than I thought you would be. David never saw this side of you, did he? No wonder he tried to keep you hidden from me."

Viola didn't respond. She used all the control she had to keep herself rooted. She pushed on her energy, sending a tap across to Casey and William. She didn't know how long she had, but she wanted them to know she was still alive. She scrabbled again with her energy to find a small sliver to pull a protective barrier over herself as she sank to the floor. The blood, his blood, seeped into her clothes. She pulled her top over her head as she began to rip it into strips.

"You won't be able to save him," Matthew said to her back.

Viola ignored him as she continued to work. Her fury channelled into her concentration. The energy she was using to heal him, she used to check the wound. The bullet had left his body, but she could feel the tears left behind. She allowed it to heal again. It wouldn't be enough, but she couldn't let this moment pass.

"You have no idea what I'm capable of." Venom dripped from her voice as she turned on the man behind her. "Your worst mistake was missing your target. Your second worst was letting me know you were descended."

She searched out for an unfamiliar magic and felt the barest sensation of something coming from Matthew. She latched her own to it and pulled it into herself. With the extra power, she concentrated on the gun Matthew had concealed again and yanked it towards her. Once she had it in her grasp, she willed her energy around it. The gun crumpled in her hands.

Matthew stared. "How did you do that?" He seemed unsteady on his feet.

Viola threw the mangled metal to the side. With one hand on David, compressing his wound, she closed her eyes and flooded her connection to the coven with the protection. Adrenaline surged through her. Images of the coven flashed across her mind, the majority focusing on her mum and her friends, as she followed the pattern her dad had left behind. She felt a small tug on the energy under her skin. She ignored it. She concentrated and used her link to Matthew to strengthen the protection. She felt the coven's link under the weaving she had put together and fused the two, completing the step her dad hadn't been able to.

A wind-like sensation rushed past her, pushing past Matthew and knocking him off his feet. The energy continued to move away from her. She dropped her connection to it as she made her way to the man who tried to kill her. His eyes widened as she loomed over him.

"You won't be able to hurt any of us now." The words sounded hollow and distant to her ears. "You missed your chance."

With a final pull of her energy, she ripped everything she could from him. The horror on his face was the last thing she saw before the world went black.

✳✳✳✳✳✳✳✳✳✳✳✳✳✳

"Viola…can you…" The words floated past her. They pulled at her. She didn't want to respond.

"Viola." There was a sensation along her arm. Her

eyes betrayed her need to ignore what was happening as they opened.

"Thank the gods you're okay." Casey leaned over her.

Bright lights dazzled her vision. She blinked as she tried to adjust to the white. Her arm ached, tubes and wires spilling from her veins. A rhythmic beeping slowly became more apparent as her vision focused on where she was.

"We didn't know who was hurt. We made them bring all of you. I'm so sorry we couldn't get there in time."

"Couldn't get there in time?" The words rasped from her throat. As quick as they left her mouth, the memories fell upon her. "Where is he?" she asked as she struggled to get up.

"Hey, take it easy," Casey said as she pushed her back into the bed. "He's being looked after. They had to rush him into theatre to deal with the wound in his stomach." Viola relaxed. "But I'm not sure how they will react to a wound like that healing without any help."

"I couldn't let him die. He stopped a bullet hitting me."

"Why?"

"He didn't take the witches; he was trying to keep us safe. It was his dad." Viola coughed as she finished speaking. "How long have I been out for?"

Casey refused look at her.

"Casey, please?"

"A day, give or take." She looked back at her. "You worried us."

"A day?" Viola sank further into the bed. "Where's

my mum? Does she know I'm okay?"

"She left to pick up some things from the house. She'll kick herself when she realises you woke up."

"As long as she's not worrying." The words slurred from her mouth.

"Sleep. We'll wake you when she's back."

"Okay." Her eyes drifted shut as the exhaustion closed in.

Chapter Thirty-Six

A breeze rushed past Viola as she made her way down the garden path. Her hair scattered and strayed from the bun she had pulled it into. Her eyes closed, a smile spreading across her face as she made the final steps towards the door.

She raised her hand to the door, moments from knocking, when it opened up. Casey's smiling face greeted her.

"The Great Viola Everett, on time for a meeting."

"The one and only." Viola smiled. "Do you need any help setting up?"

"We're almost done, but I'm sure Abigail won't mind you coming in early."

Casey held the door wide for Viola to step in. Warmth spread over Viola as she made her way inside.

"Good afternoon, Viola," Ms. Glorian called to her as she entered the living room.

"Afternoon," she responded. "Casey said you didn't

need any help, but I know she's too polite to ask at times."

"We're all set up, but if you want to soundproof the room, it would help."

"Of course."

Viola's magic jumped at her touch. It filled out and spread across her hands. She let it twist and spread through the room as the soundproofing began. A small tug pulled her attention to the kitchen. Casey nodded her head into the doorway.

"Let me check if it's worked."

"I am confident in your abilities, Viola."

"Thank you, but I want to make sure."

Viola followed Casey's presence into the kitchen. A cup of tea waited for her on the side.

"How are you?"

"I'm good." She took a drink of the hot liquid, enjoying the burn as it slid down her throat. "I mean it."

Her friend looked at her with concern. "No, how are you really? We've barely spoken, and you haven't been practising."

"How did you— oh, the joining." Viola sighed. "I've been better. Everything happened so quickly. I don't know if I've come to terms with everything yet. I'm sure I'll be fine."

"Vi, you could have died."

"But I didn't."

"Not for lack of trying," Casey said wryly. "You don't need to hide from me. I meant it before; we're in this together."

"Thanks."

Silence dropped around them. Casey fidgeted.

"You can ask."

"How is he?" The words came out quiet, small.

"He's good. A lot better than a couple of weeks ago."

"Does he remember what happened?"

"Some of it. I don't want to go into too many details. He knows his dad died, but he's fuzzy on why he was in the hospital."

"You will tell him, though?"

"I wouldn't keep it from him. He's apologised for not telling me the truth, and I've apologised for ghosting him. But he understands why I did it."

"I'm happy for you both." Casey hugged her. "Come on, I think people are starting to turn up."

William waved them over to a couple of chairs as they walked back into the living room. They sat with him as they listened to the announcements from the Elders. Viola couldn't feel the energies buzzing around her. They were quiet. More relaxed than she had ever felt them. It had been a few weeks, but the feeling of safety and security still surprised her. The protection wasn't the same as her dad had put in place. It had evolved, and this time it would stay.

Acknowledgements

The idea for Arcane Connection came to me as I was finishing the edits of Artefact 299. It was the middle of the Covid-19 lockdowns and I felt like I had all the time in the world to write. When I felt like trying to write a story between a nurse and a film star. David quickly changed into a business tycoon, but the original vibes still stand.

I wanted to try something a little bit different, but also familiar to me. I've always loved fantasy stories so I made my nurse into a witch and Viola was born. I did try to make it more into a romance, but I didn't feel like their ending would be as happy as everyone wanted. Sorry if you were wanting something more upbeat but just know their story doesn't end with complete disaster.

I wouldn't have been able to get this book if it wasn't for Turner Edits and Alpha for providing an Alpha read for me, Karen Sanders Editing for completing the line and copy edits and, Proofreading by Mich to complete those final checks.

As always, thank you to Todd for helping to keep me on track and being my rubber duck for ideas. Also, thank you for making sure Violet has given me the peace I needed to get those final touches done.

Viola's story feels almost like home to me now and I hope you have enjoyed reading her story as much as I did writing it.

About the Author

L.A. Binley is a science fiction and fantasy writer. She has a BA Hons in French and Spanish from Bangor University in North Wales. Although it was mainly as an excuse to travel, she believes it has helped with her grammar. Editors are still to be convinced.

When not withering away in front of her computer, she likes to practice her French and Spanish through the medium of song.

To find out more about L.A. Binley head to her website below:

https://labinley.com

Newsletter

Want to hear more from me? Head to https://labinley.
com/newsletter to sign up to my monthly newsletter.
Including sneak peaks for any future projects!